SHERLOCK HOLMES
MYSTERY MAGAZINE

VOL. 6, NO. 2   Issue #17

Publisher: John Betancourt
Editor: Marvin Kaye
Non-fiction Editor: Carla Coupe
Assistant Editor: Steve Coupe

Sherlock Holmes Mystery Magazine is published by Wildside Press, LLC. Single copies: $10.00 + $3.00 postage. U.S. subscriptions: $59.95 (postage paid) for the next 6 issues in the U.S.A., from: Wildside Press LLC, Subscription Dept. 9710 Traville Gateway Dr., #234; Rockville MD 20850. International subscriptions: see our web site at www.wildsidemagazines.com. Available as an ebook through all major ebook etailers, or our web site, www.wildsidemagazines.com.

FROM WATSON'S SCRAPBOOK

In this issue of *Sherlock Holmes Mystery Magazine,* I am pleased to present my account of the case of "The Greek Interpreter." It was one of my friend's decided triumphs, but it is, I think, especially interesting because it introduces for the first time in the chronicles that Holmesians call "the Canon" the large figure of Holmes's older brother Mycroft.

When first I met him, I understood that he examined the account-books for Great Britain, although later I discovered that at times Mycroft Holmes' advice was so critical to the running of our government that, according to Sherlock, he *was* the power to be reckoned with. And yet, he was the laziest industrious person imaginable!

His size and girth may have been partly the reason for this. He was so very stout (I should say *is*, for he never retired) that moving anywhere was quite the effort. When he was not labouring at Whitehall, he spent most of his time at that peculiar institution, the Diogenes Club, where speaking aloud is forbidden except in the visitor's chamber.

Mycroft Holmes became involved in other of his brother's adventures, and in due time those cases will be presented in the pages of this periodical.

And now for a few words from my friend and colleague, Mr Kaye.

–John H Watson, M D

✗　✗　✗　✗

In this issue, I am pleased to feature two fascinating articles. Peter James Quirk tells the story of Eddie Chapman, a career criminal who, turning straight, became Great Britain's most valuable spy during the Second World War. Another criminal is the subject of "Brooklyn's Elusive Mr. G." by Albert Ashford. Harry Gross may just be history's—or at least Brooklyn's—most likeable criminal. His exploits are both startling and amazing, and Mr. Ashford's recounting of Mr. G.'s life and career is quite knowledgeable since the author's family knew and liked him very much. Mr. Ashford even met Mr. G. on at least one occasion.

At least three authors appearing here have been in earlier issues: Steve Liskow, Laird Long, and Steve Hagood. The newcomers include R. J. Lewis, Alex Shvartsman, and Kim Newman.

Next time will feature stories by "recidivists" Carole Buggé, Janice Law, Steve Liskow, and Laird Long, as well as Cenydd Ros, Zakariah Johnson (a new Sherlock Holmes case), and Steven Shrott.

Canonically Yours,
Marvin Kaye

COMING NEXT TIME...

STORIES! ARTICLES!
SHERLOCK HOLMES & DR. WATSON!

*Sherlock Holmes Mystery Magazine #18
is just a few months away...watch for it!*

Not a subscriber yet?
Send $59.95 for 6 issues (postage paid in the U.S.) to:

**Wildside Press LLC
Attn: Subscription Dept.
9710 Traville Gateway Dr. #234
Rockville MD 20850**

You can also subscribe online at
www.wildsidemagazines.com

ASK MRS HUDSON

by (Mrs) Martha Hudson

Dear Mrs H –

I wonder whether you know of any cases that Mr Holmes failed to solve?

Curious in Chesterfield

✗   ✗   ✗

Dear Curious (Mr or Mrs, I wonder) –

If you have been following Dr Watson's adventures in this magazine, you will be aware that one such failure was reported in the preceding issue. I heard my tenants discussing with some heat the appearance of the story in those pages; Mr Holmes did not want it to be reprinted *ever*. But eventually Dr Watson wore him down, with the proviso that the issue not be left laying about in the apartment. (Personally, I have not yet read the tale because my subscription always arrives late, thanks to it coming from somewhere in America, Mary-land I think it is called.)

Other than the problem cited above, there is only one time I recollect my tenant committing what he called a "grievous error." Mr Holmes has an excellent memory, but it did not work this once and as a result he forgot to send a birthday greeting to Inspector Lestrade, of Scotland Yard. Yes, I imagine hearing this is a bit surprising; the two investigators were often at odds with one another. But Holmes actually rather liked the Inspector "despite his faults," as he put it. (Dr Watson was rather fond of Lestrade; he ran into him by chance one evening and they shared libations together.)

Well, Mr Holmes did something he'd never before done: he sent the Inspector a present in the form of two tickets for Lestrade and his wife to whichever Gilbert & Sullivan operetta was then playing at the Savoy.

Yours Truly,

Mrs Hudson

✗   ✗   ✗   ✗

Dear Mrs Hudson,

Did any of Mr Holmes's adventures ever put you in danger?

Worried on Your Behalf

✗   ✗   ✗

Dear Worried –

That is ever so thoughtful of you, so let me reassure you that I have never been at risk because of Mr Holmes's doings.

However, there is one time that I experienced some minor discomfort because of what was frankly (and he admitted it) his carelessness. Here is what happened: Mr Holmes had just quitted the premises (Dr Watson was still abed). His friend had been working with chemicals that morning and when he left, I entered the room and nearly choked on the abominable stink. I hastened to open the windows and let in some much-needed fresh air…

The next thing I knew, a sharp pungent odour assailed my nostrils. My eyes were shut; they popped open and I realized that I was on my back on the floor and that Dr Watson was kneeling beside me holding smelling salts to my nose. I winced and sneezed and sat up. "What on earth happened?" I demanded.

"I don't know, Mrs H, but this is how I found you when I came in a few moments ago. You appear to have passed out."

It all came back to me in a rush. I explained the circumstances, and the good doctor insisted that I go to my room and lay down for a time, which I did straightaway.

Later, Mr Holmes rapped at my door and apologized profusely. "Watson has raked me over the coals quite thoroughly. I should have cracked open a window, but it was a bit chilly, so I did not do so. I am, therefore, wholly to blame."

I got to my feet. "It was just an accident. Now if you'll excuse me, I will begin to prepare luncheon for you and Dr Watson."

He shook his head vigorously. "Absolutely not. You will be my guest at Rumplemeyer's, you and Watson, of course."

I did not argue. That was a new and expensive restaurant that I'd heard was splendid. And it was!

Yours truly,

Mrs Hudson

Dear Mrs Hudson,

For a few months the other year, you traveled to Yorkshire to nurse your ailing Aunt Ruth. I do hope she is now well?

Professor Alvin Tupper

My Dear Professor,

I am happy to report that she is considerably improved, though her disposition is always a bit weak, I am afraid. But she has a dear companion who looks after her, and I wonder if you are related to one another, for his name is Algernon Tupper. (I later that they are cousins, but have never met.)

Mr Tupper actually became one of Mr Holmes's clients some time ago. A valuable old coin collection of Mr Tupper's was stolen and by way of my aunt, I prevailed upon Mr Holmes to help him. He did so, but would not tell me the details, only that the coins had been recovered and the perpetrator was fully penitent. I did learn, at least, that Mr Tupper was in great financial difficulties at that time, which made me suspicious, but Mr Holmes entreated me not to pursue the matter, nor mention it to my aunt. This I agreed to, though it persuaded me that poor Mr Tupper had pretended to have been robbed, in hopes of obtaining insurance monies.

This much more Mr Holmes shared with me. "Tupper is quite the innocent," the detective averred. "He is a British Army veteran, but had no idea that he could collect a pension for his services. I spoke to my brother about this, and he arranged not only for the pension to be paid immediately, but to include a sizable sum con-stituting uncollected benefits. Mr Tupper was wounded in action, so the reward cleared him of all fiscal problems."

I knew privately that he had one other problem, but it was quite unsolvable. He wished to marry my aunt, but never had the nerve to ask her—which is just as well, for I do not think she would have accepted, much as she is fond of him. She is just not the marrying kind.

Yours Truly,
Mrs Hudson

Dear Mrs Hudson,

I am a professional chef in New York City. I am an avid subscriber to *Sherlock Holmes Mystery Magazine* and always look forward to the recipes you elect to share with the readers.

I have three kitchen-related questions.

1. Has Mr Holmes's brother Mycroft ever dined at Baker Street, and if so, what did he consume, and did he like it?

2. What cuisine is Dr Watson fond of? Is there anything he does not like?

3. I repeat the above question *anent* Mr Holmes.

Good Appetite,

Randolph Brenner

✗   ✗   ✗

Dear Mr Brenner,

I am delighted at your questions!

Mycroft Holmes dined with us last spring. It was the only time, so far at least. I served my rack of lamb with fresh vegetables, salad, and trifle for dessert. He enjoyed everything; I doubt that there is any food he dislikes. I base this, in part, on the gentleman's *size*.

Dr Watson is never a fussy eater. He is not fond of brussel sprouts, so I seldom serve them, but since Mr Holmes likes them, they appear occasionally at the table. The doctor has graciously observed that the way I prepare them "is the only way I can get them down."

There is one food-stuff, however, that Dr Watson detests, so I always prepare him something else to eat when I serve shad roe. Mr Holmes, you see, is quite fond of it, and apparently so is his brother. Personally, I do not care for it, either, but I have provided my recipe for it below.

Finally, Mr Holmes is himself a gourmet, and though Dr Watson is not aware of it, his friend likes to do things in the kitchen from time to time. He has a marvelous "duckling surprise," the surprise being that there is no duck in it. When Dr Watson tasted it, thinking, of course, that I'd made it, he was ecstatic, and said I had surpassed myself and it was the finest duckling he'd ever tasted.

One last thing: at breakfast, both of the gentlemen are quite fond of shirred eggs, but I do not make them often, for they are a bit time-consuming… which is why, I believe, few restaurants offer them. The word shirred itself, I understand, comes from the kind of shallow baking dish in which the eggs are prepared. At any rate, I include my recipe for them below.

Yours Truly,
Mrs Hudson

⚔ ⚔ ⚔ ⚔

SHAD ROE CASSEROLE

2 shad roe
4 tablespoons of anchovy butter
lard
1 teaspoon of onion, minced
1 teaspoon of chervil
2 tablespoons of shallots, finely chopped
1 teaspoon of marjoram
1 bay leaf
salt and pepper, as desired
1½ cups of heavy cream

Directions:
1. Heat oven to 375 degrees.
2. Rinse shad roe in salted water.
3. Spread anchovy butter on the shad roe.
4. Roll the roe in lard, securing with string, if necessary.
5. Add all of the spices.
6. Add the cream and cover the dish.
7. Bake for half an hour.
8. Uncover the dish and bake for five more minutes.
9. Before serving from the casserole, cover it with the sauce.

⚔ ⚔ ⚔ ⚔

SHIRRED EGGS FOR TWO

4 eggs
2 tablespoons of light cream
Salt, pepper, and paprika, as desired.
Chives
Butter

Directions:
1. Heat oven to 325 degrees.
2. Paint butter over two baking dishes.
3. Add 1 tablespoon of cream to each dish.
4. Crack two eggs into each dish, making sure not to break them.
5. Sprinkle with salt, pepper, and paprika.
6. Bake for 12 to 20 minutes, depending on taste.
7. Add minced chives to each set of eggs and serve.

HIS LATEST BOW:

William Gillette in *Sherlock Holmes*

reviewed by Timothy S. Greer

BASSICK: *Sherlock Holmes? Again?*
MORIARTY: *And again. And again. And again.*

–*from* Sherlock Holmes
by William Gillette and A. Conan Doyle

One of the century's greatest Sherlockian discoveries, the 1916 film *Sherlock Holmes*, starring William Gillette, turns out to be a long-deferred delight. Sherlockians from around the world responded exuberantly to the restoration's U.S. premiere at the San Francisco Silent Film Festival in May, held at the city's historic Castro Theatre.

The plot—involving blackmail letters, Moriarty, and a scheme to assassinate Holmes—closely adheres to Gillette's celebrated 1899 play of the same title, itself based on "A Scandal in Bohemia" and "The Final Problem." Impressive camera moves enliven Arthur Berthelet's otherwise-routine direction, and, outside the walls of Essanay Studios, cobblestoned Chicago exteriors double effectively for London and its environs. The supporting cast is a bit uneven in strength, but not distractingly so, with the strongest support coming from Edward Fielding as Dr. Watson and Burford Hampden as Billy.

The main attraction is, of course, the great detective himself, and Gillette is razor-sharp as Sherlock Holmes. Still in fine form at age 62, and easily passing for a much younger man, he remains a snarky and charismatic lead. His trademark "long silences"—suspenseful scenes without dialogue that showcased his remarkable gifts as a physical actor—are tailor-made for silent cinema. In these sequences, his performance electrifies. Also of interest are several visual tropes familiar to viewers of later Sherlockian adaptations:

The phrenology head from CBS's *Elementary*? Gillette had it first. The "skull friend" from the BBC's *Sherlock*? Check.

For fans of Holmes, silent films, or both, *Sherlock Holmes* is not to be missed. Flicker Alley releases the film to DVD and Blu-ray on 20 October 2015.

Timothy S. Greer teaches Detective Fiction, Shakespeare, and other subjects in Memphis, TN, where he is a member of the scion The Giant Rats of Sumatra. He won the Morley-Montgomery Award for his article "Murger in Baker Street" in the Autumn 2014 issue of *The Baker Street Journal*.

AN UNLIKELY HERO:

THE TRUE STORY OF THE ROGUE WHO BECAME BRITAIN'S MOST VALUABLE SPY

by Peter James Quirk

1

On June 30, 1940, in the early days of World War II, the German army invaded the British Channel Islands and began their five-year occupation of the only part of Great Britain that came under Nazi control during that apocalyptic conflict.

These islands, located just a few miles from the coast of Normandy, France, became part of Great Britain when William the Conqueror, Duke of Normandy, invaded England and defeated and killed King Harold at the Battle of Hastings in 1066 and assumed the English throne as King William I. And although England managed to lose almost all its other French possessions during the Hundred Years War, they somehow held onto the Channel Islands, an extremely popular English vacation destination for many years.

Incarcerated on the Island of Jersey at the time was a twenty-five-year-old career criminal named Edward Arnold (Eddie) Chapman. Eddie, born in the early days of World War I in a small village in the coal fields of Northern England, was unloved and unsupervised as a boy and routinely cut school to spend his afternoons at the movies in the nearby town of Sunderland.

When his school days were over, and after several dead-end jobs, Eddie moved south to London to join the Coldstream Guards at the age of seventeen. He lasted nine months. When granted his first leave, he gravitated to Soho in London's West End, which in the 1930's was a hot bed of drama, passion and exotic night clubs—a melting pot where celebrities rubbed shoulders with ladies of the night, pimps, and underworld villains.

All this was tremendously exciting to an impressionable teenager and Eddie, who immediately lost his virginity to the first girl who caught his eye, became captivated by the lifestyle and stayed with the girl for two months. He was eventually arrested for desertion and thrown into the stockade, where he served three months hard labor and received a dishonorable discharge. He went straight back to Soho, where the atmosphere perfectly suited his outgoing personality and dubious character.

At the time Eddie Chapman was eighteen—tall, slim, with a pencil-thin Errol Flynn moustache and naturally gregarious—all of which made him popular with members of both sexes. He supported himself by working variously as a bartender, masseur, movie extra, boxer and wrestler, all the while acquiring an extremely indulgent and extravagant lifestyle.

When his money ran out, Eddie turned to crime and for the next several years he survived as a small-time burglar, for which he served several short prison terms. Then two things happened at roughly the same time: the criminal underworld discovered an explosive called gelignite and Eddie met a highly-skilled safe-cracker named Jimmy Hunt during one of his jail terms. They formed an alliance with two other petty thieves that came to be known to Scotland Yard as the Jelly Gang.

The Jelly Gang was a quite successful enterprise for some time and Eddie, with money in his pockets, began mixing with celebrities and intellectuals. To keep up with their conversation, he began reading widely and even married a half-Russian, half-German-Jewish girl named Vera, who taught him German. This marriage, however, didn't prevent him from impregnating a stage dancer named Freda.

And when police finally caught up with Chapman and his Jelly Gang associates, they were hiding out in the Channel Isles. Indeed, Eddie was in a restaurant with Betty Farmer, yet another girl brought with him from England, when he noticed detectives arrive. He promptly said goodbye to his new lover, leapt straight through a picture window and began running along the beach, closely followed by the police.

Chapman managed to escape arrest that evening, but found himself on an unfamiliar island with little ready cash, which he immediately remedied by breaking into a local public building.

And although this appeared an incredibly stupid move since he still had nowhere to hide and nowhere to go, it turned out to be an enormous stroke of luck. When the other members of the gang were extradited back to England to begin long prison sentences, Eddie, because he had broken the law in Jersey, first had to serve a term in the island jail. And that was where he sat when Britain declared war on Nazi Germany in September, 1939.

By the time the *Wehrmacht* arrived in the Channel Islands to begin its occupation, Eddie, a restless soul who was easily bored, had read every book in the prison library twice, begun improving his German as well as studying French, and had escaped from prison and been recaptured. When he was finally released from the island jail some two years later, he immediately ran afoul of the occupying army by colliding with a Nazi officer in the street—they were both on bicycles and unbeknownst to Eddie, the Nazis switched the traffic flow on the Islands's roads from the British left to the Continental right.

Eddie Chapman, who was now dabbling in the black market, was seen as a trouble maker, so when resistance fighters began cutting telephone lines on the island, the Nazis arrested him immediately (the only time he was ever detained for an offense for which he was completely innocent), but this time he was incarcerated, not in Jersey, but in the Fort de Romainville, a notorious medieval fortress-prison in Paris, a prison from which there was no escape.

Romainville held prisoners of all stripes, mostly civilians who displeased the new masters of France in some way: Resistance fighters, Jews, communists, or hostages male and female; Romainville was a huge holding tank. If any Nazi soldier was assassinated, prisoners from Romainville were selected to be executed in reprisal. As a political prisoner and suspected saboteur, Eddie joined the mix and even managed couplings with female prisoners, a dangerous undertaking that was strictly forbidden.

One of Eddie's schemes to escape from the Jersey prison had been to send a letter to the Nazi Command volunteering himself as a spy. Nothing had come of this at the time, and Eddie had completely forgotten about it until, four months after arriving at the Fort de Romainville, he was pulled from solitary confinement to interview for *Abwehr* (the German Secret Service). And in the spring of 1942, after four years of almost continuous incarceration,

Eddie Chapman was transferred to La Villa de la Bretonnière, a spy training camp in Nantes, in north-western France.

This was an enormous step up from the deprivations and beatings Eddie had received at Romainville. He now had a room with a comfortable bed, clean sheets and, more importantly, an unlocked door. He also fraternized easily with his spy trainers and superiors and became especially close to the Commandant, a German aristocrat named Stephan von Gröning, who Eddie knew as Dr. Graumann. All this camaraderie, however, didn't prevent Eddie from collecting information he knew would be valuable to the British, if and when he was ever sent to England. And to assist him in this endeavor, he worked hard to improve both his German and his French.

Eddie Chapman's training progressed throughout 1942 with only one impediment, a setback that almost killed him. This occurred during his parachute training at a small airport near Paris: Eddie's first jump went off without a hitch, but his parachute failed to open properly on his second. He landed badly and required massive reconstruction work on his jaw and teeth (paid for by *Abwehr*).

2

Despite this injury and other distractions—the entire complement of La Bretonière was enlisted to assist in the invasion and occupation of Vichy France in November 1942—Fritz, Eddie's *Abwehr* code name, completed his training early in December. And before dawn on the morning of December 16, 1942, Eddie parachuted into East Anglia, a large area of fertile farmland north and east of London. His mission: to sabotage an airplane manufacturing plant just north of London.

This facility built the De Havilland Mosquito; an aircraft that had become a thorn in the side of the *Luftwaffe* and its leader, Air *Reichsmarschall* Hermann Göring. The Mosquito was an extremely light wooden airplane with a top speed in excess of four hundred miles per hour that could outrun any German fighter plane even when carrying two tons of bombs. It was very effective for bombing specific sites such as *Gestapo* headquarters in various cities and could be constructed simply and inexpensively by carpenters and cabinet makers.

Of course, Eddie Chapman had no intention of carrying out this assignment. He simply knocked on the first farmhouse he found and called the police, although, much to his annoyance, he had difficulty getting the officer on duty to take him seriously. By the end of the day, however, he was in London being debriefed by MI5 (the British Secret Service).

By the end of 1942, the pendulum of war was just beginning to swing back toward Britain, thanks in no small part to a coterie of mathematicians and scientists now known as the Bletchley code breakers. This highly secretive group and their assistants, usually secretaries and bookkeepers and almost always women, worked tirelessly to break all the Nazi radio codes: chiefly Enigma, the code used by the Nazi military machine. The Nazis believed Enigma unbreakable, and continued to do so until the end of the war.

Bletchley also allowed MI5 to listen in to all *Abwehr* communications, so they were well aware that a superspy, code named Fritz and probably British-born, was on his way to England, although they had no idea of his true identity and didn't believe they had much chance of catching him. If they were able to apprehend him, they had a standard procedure concerning captured enemy spies; they were offered a simple choice: become a double agent and work for MI5 or to dangle at the end of a rope. Very few chose the latter, since spies by nature are not drawn to that profession by feelings of intense patriotism, but rather because they crave adventure and excitement.

With Eddie Chapman they had a somewhat different situation. Eddie was willing, indeed eager, to work with them and brought valuable information about *Abwehr* and its workings to prove it. There was, however, an open warrant for his arrest as a founding member of the infamous Jelly Gang, and if picked up by the police, he was looking at a prison sentence of at least ten to fifteen years.

At the time, MI5 was staffed by mostly upper-middle class Cambridge University graduates. These men, usually members of private men's clubs, would have nothing in common with a poorly educated, street-smart villain. They did have a common goal, however, and that was to win the war at all costs. In Eddie, MI5 had a valuable instrument to achieve just that. It didn't hurt that Eddie was a good conversationalist, well read in three languages and, thanks to his *Abwehr* training, an expert in radio transmission and sabotage techniques.

They placed Eddie in a safe house in North London watched over by two former policemen and minded by a radio and technology expert, Captain Ronnie Reed, who would monitor his communications with *Abwehr*. (Eddie and Reed would become very close as the war progressed.) To ensure that Fritz remained valuable to Germany, MI5 faked an explosion at the De Havilland factory, orchestrated by a famous music-hall magician, whose sleight-of-hand had recently helped the British win the battle of El Alamein in North Africa. To keep Eddie loyal to MI5 and tame his restless spirit and equally restless libido, they found the dancer Freda and moved her into the safe house with Eddie's three-year-old daughter, whom he had never previously met.

The Nazi regime was jubilant on learning of the successful attack on the De Havilland factory by a German saboteur (Eddie was eventually awarded the Iron Cross, the only Englishman ever to receive this award) and consequently *Abwehr* was in no hurry to bring him back to the Continent. MI5, however, wished to send their new secret weapon back to start creating havoc behind enemy lines as soon as possible. This sentiment was endorsed by Eddie, who by now was intoxicated by the rush that came with his clandestine missions. He even proposed and outlined a credible plan to assassinate Hitler, which was much debated but eventually vetoed, possibly by Churchill himself.

In May 1942, British-trained Czech operatives assassinated a high-ranking Nazi, one of the architects of the holocaust, Reinhard Heydrich. But the reprisals were so barbaric—a Czech village, Lidice, reputed to be home to one of the assassins, was razed to the ground, all men and boys from the age of sixteen were executed and the women and children deported to Nazi concentration camps to die—that the British Government discouraged further assassination attempts.

In February 1943, Eddie, with MI5's assistance, concocted an emergency that included the arrest of his "assistant," Jimmy Hunt—who was safely in prison and had been for years—and sent a final radio message to *Abwehr* saying he was closing down transmissions and that he would attempt to make it back through Lisbon.

3

MI5 promptly went to work on a plan to make that happen. They fed Chapman with a plausible story of Fritz's time in England, and then grilled him for hours as though they were Nazi interrogators until he knew it by heart—they even gave him a list of not-too-damaging information to give to *Abwehr* that included the address of the Inland Revenue Service (the British income tax headquarters). They then inserted him as a crew member on a cargo ship that was due to stop at Lisbon. Nobody on the ship, the MV *City of Lancaster*, knew Eddie's true identity except the captain, Reginald Kearon, a fearless Irishman who had already lost two ships to the ever-present U-boat menace.

On March 15, 1943, the *City of Lancaster* sailed to Lisbon as part of a convoy, a convoy that in two days and nights lost seven ships to U-boats and the *Luftwaffe*. Needless to say, Assistant Steward Hugh Anson, Chapman's temporary *nom de guerre,* between the attacks and his own constant seasickness, did not get much sleep. And because he had been advised by the captain to complain constantly, thus giving him a reason to jump ship, he was not exactly popular with his Liverpool-Irish shipmates.

Two days later, the *City of Lancaster* docked in Lisbon and Eddie went to work trying to contact the local *Abwehr*. Eventually he was sent to someone who seemed familiar with who he was. Fritz immediately offered to blow up the *City of Lancaster* by using a camouflaged bomb (this device was a bomb disguised as a lump of coal that could be thrown into the fuel supply and would sink the ship when it was shoveled into the boiler), something Eddie knew *Abwehr* had access to. Of course, MI5 was alerted to his proposition—thanks to the Bletchley code breakers—and immediately went into a tailspin, believing their prize spy had switched sides once again.

Eddie, however, had a different plan, and just before he jumped ship, he gave the coal bomb to Captain Kearon with instructions to deliver it to MI5 when he arrived back in Liverpool. He also picked a fight with a burly crew member, which gave him yet another excuse for wanting to jump ship—starting a fight on a ship in wartime was a criminal offence subject to jail time. And as soon as the *City of Lancaster* left port, Eddie, sporting a huge black eye from a head butt that ended the fight, reported for duty at the Lisbon headquarters of *Abwehr*.

After weeks of debriefing and interrogation, Eddie eventually was sent to Oslo, where he was reunited with his old commandant, Stephan von Gröning. Von Gröning had been serving on the Eastern front, but was brought back at Eddie's request, for which he was extremely grateful. Consequently, Eddie lived very well during his stay in Norway and although he was consulted occasionally on matters of espionage and sabotage, he was basically on hold until a new sabotage mission could be found.

One consequence of his sojourn in Norway was that he fell completely off the MI5 grid. Indeed, the common consensus at MI5 HQ was that he had been exposed and executed. They needn't have been concerned. Iron Cross recipient Fritz was spending the summer sailing up and down Norwegian fjords with his new girlfriend Dagmar, also Norwegian, all the while mapping out potential targets for the RAF (the British Air Force). This included the palatial home of Vidkun Quisling, the Norwegian Nazi who sold out his country to Hitler and whose name even now is synonymous with treachery.

At some point that summer, Eddie was called upon to teach radio technology and the Morse code to two eager but inept Icelandic Nazis who had been recruited to set up a spy network in their homeland. These men showed absolutely zero aptitude for their assignment, and were captured—already almost frozen to death—within forty-eight hours of being put ashore on a remote part of the island.

When they were sent to London to be questioned by MI5, their interrogators were astonished when these deluded Icelanders described the high-ranking member of *Abwehr* who taught them the Morse code. MI5 showed them photos of Eddie and they both agreed that this was the spy-master who had been their instructor. And so MI5 learned to their absolute delight that Zigzag, Eddie's MI5 code name, was alive and well and living in Oslo, although what he was doing there was anyone's guess.

In the meantime, Nazi High Command was finding assignments for Fritz: the German Navy, that for years had been destroying massive numbers of Allied shipping in the North Atlantic with their U-boats, was finding that the British were now beginning to sink these boats in large numbers. In May 1943, alone, some forty U-boats were sunk, killing more than a thousand German sailors; High Command wanted to know the how and the why of this turn-around.

They were convinced that Britain had developed a form of underwater radar that even allowed them to discover U-boats sitting with silent engines on the ocean floor. But the truth, of course, was much simpler. They were being traced through their radio transmissions, which, thanks to Bletchley and their breaking of the Enigma code, the Royal Navy could read at will, and track to their source. It would be Eddie's dubious mission to find this mysterious underwater radar system and bring the plans back to Berlin.

The *Luftwaffe* had a similar mission: British fighter planes were slowly taking command of the night sky, thanks to a night radar system known as AI 10 developed in the United States. And although the *Luftwaffe* had shot down planes with the system installed, not enough of the radar was salvaged to understand how it worked. Fritz, of course, was just the man to filch a copy of the plans and get them to Nazi High Command.

As fighting progressed through 1943, the Allies conquered North Africa and turned their sights toward Sicily, and the Soviets turned Hitler's eastern army at Stalingrad. All of which gave Nazi High Command reason to suspect that they might lose the war. In their desperate minds, super-spy Fritz's espionage skills were growing exponentially. The orders given to him before his return to England were to capture the plans of the two types of radar, then steal a motor boat and rendezvous with German sea planes in the North Sea, ten miles off the English coast. Stealing a sea-worthy boat in wartime England would have been close to impossible, but Eddie raised no objections; he simply prepared to be dropped once again over his homeland.

4

In the spring of 1944, Eddie Chapman went with von Gröning to Berlin—which by this time had been devastated by British bombing raids—to receive his final instructions. And it was there he first learned of the new unmanned flying bombs he was told both sides were developing. Finding out how far the British had progressed with this fearsome new weapon was simply the latest task to be added to Fritz's list of assignments.

The two men then traveled to Paris to find transportation to England. This proved to be extremely difficult and Eddie was still in Paris waiting for a flight on June 6, when the D-day assault forces fought their way onto the beaches of Normandy. This momentous invasion irrevocably altered the course of the war and changed Eddie's mission once again.

A week after D-day, the first unmanned flying bombs, the fearsome V-1 rockets, began landing on London. MI5 immediately sought to minimize the effects of these terrible bombs by dismissing the damage as slight in daily news reports. And although more than six thousand civilians would be killed by these bombs—known to Londoners as doodlebugs—over the next two months, it was hoped that if the Nazis didn't know where they were falling and what damage they were doing, the attacks would be deemed a failure. To counter this lack of information, *Abwehr* would send the ever-reliable Fritz to become their eyes and ears.

On the morning of June 29, 1944, two weeks after the first doodlebugs struck the British capital, super-spy Fritz floated down once again over the fertile farms of East Anglia. He was carrying a suitcase full of espionage equipment, a herculean list of assignments, and an enormous hangover. The latter was courtesy of a going-away party thrown for him in Paris by his spy-master von Gröning and attended by several high-ranking Nazis. No matter that the Allies were fast bearing down upon Paris from the Normandy coast; Fritz, their secret weapon and possibly their last chance for ultimate victory, needed an appropriate send-off.

Again, Eddie had difficulty convincing the local police that he was a British agent newly arrived from Europe, but by the end of the day all was well and he was back in MI5 headquarters. And two days later—after extensive debriefing by MI5's top interrogators—Fritz sent his first radio message to *Abwehr* signaling his arrival.

Of all the problems facing MI5, the flying bombs that threatened to destroy London was the most immediate. These doodlebugs arrived overhead, their engines making an eerie droning sound, until they ran out of fuel and dropped silently and destructively upon the helpless citizenry, causing untold death and destruction.

But now by using Eddie and his radio messages, MI5 could feed the Nazis misleading information and even steer the V-1 rockets away from London and out into the countryside. This deception was reasonably successful and saved countless lives, until anti-aircraft batteries set up and manned by American forces began regularly shooting down the rockets in July, effectively ending the threat.

By this time, Eddie had been sitting at his radio tapping misleading information for over a month, and he was getting bored and restless. Although he hinted at new assignments he could be tackling behind enemy lines, MI5 had no intention of sending him back. He was much too valuable sitting in his safe house distributing lies and propaganda to the Nazis. And as such he was becoming the subject of much discussion at MI5 HQ.

The top brass of MI5 were debating how they could reward Eddie for his service, which was considerable: Eddie Chapman, albeit a wanted felon, courageously put his life on the line for his country almost daily for over two years and in doing so accomplished some amazing feats of espionage. He infiltrated the Nazi secret service and brought back immeasurable amounts of Nazi intelligence, and he saved countless British lives with his misleading radio transmissions to *Abwehr*. He also extracted roughly $10,000—over $400,000 in today's money—from the Nazi exchequer, while costing the British almost nothing.

It was finally decided that Edward Arnold Chapman should be pardoned for any and all of his British transgressions. Because he could only be pardoned for offenses for which he had already been tried and found guilty, he was given an unofficial pardon by the Home Secretary—the British Cabinet Minister responsible for the laws of the land and the police force that upheld them—that effectively lasted until the day he died. In an attempt to keep him honest, Eddie was never informed of his get-out-of-jail-free card, although it must have dawned on him eventually—he was in court some twenty times between his dismissal from MI5 and his death, but he never spent another night in prison.

MI5 began giving Eddie more freedom now that he was in no danger of arrest and he began spending a lot more time with his old underworld pals. He also had a change of handlers. His friend Ronnie Reed, the radio expert Eddie had first been assigned to, was promoted to major and sent to France to be MI5's official co-ordinator with the American Army. Eddie was so moved by losing this old friend and collaborator that he gave him his Iron Cross as a going-away present.

Unfortunately, the man who replaced Reed would prove to be Eddie's undoing. Michael Ryde was a college-educated, upper-class snob with a serious drinking problem; Eddie and he disliked each other from their first meeting. Since it was Ryde's job to be Eddie's constant companion, even when Eddie was off duty and out drinking with his underworld compatriots, mutual dislike quickly turned to loathing. Ryde went on a personal crusade to have this loutish criminal he was forced to accompany dismissed from the hallowed halls of MI5. It didn't take long.

Eddie admitted in conversation with Ryde that he knew von Gröning was skimming the reward money Fritz was receiving from *Abwehr*, which meant that they were effectively in collusion to extort money from the Nazi government. What else were they sharing? That was a momentous question in an organization like MI5, whose members were bound to be paranoid. The final blow came, however, when an MI5 messenger came looking for Eddie when he was with his pals. And Eddie's old partner in crime, Jimmy Hunt, newly released from prison, gave the messenger a knowing wink and asked if he were taking Eddie away to do a job. Here was absolute proof that Eddie hadn't maintained the secrecy required to be an effective operative. He was dismissed immediately.

On November 28, 1944, the career of one of Britain's most effective clandestine operatives ended, a man whose loyalty and courage had no equal, and whose exploits when performing his duties, drinking with his Nazi spymasters or leaving broken hearts in his wake, rivaled all other legendary heroes, whether they hailed from history books or the purple prose of fiction.

Indeed, when Eddie was working with Naval Intelligence trying to invent a super underwater radar system to sell to the Nazis, it is very possible that he met Ian Fleming, the creator of "shaken not stirred." Fleming worked with British Naval Intelligence the entire war, and the Bond stories and movies would have been a fitting epitaph for a complex and paradoxical man like Eddie Chapman.

But shed no tears for Eddie. Soon after his abrupt dismissal from MI5, Eddie went into business with Billy Hill, the self-styled king of the London underworld, just in time for the post-war years, which in England offered untold opportunities for men with larceny in their hearts. Eddie also went looking for—and found—the girl he left in the restaurant in Jersey when he dove through the picture window to evade the police. Betty Farmer and Eddie married and lived happily until Eddie died, a rich man, at the age of eighty-four in 1997. At the time, they owned a castle in Ireland and a successful spa not far from the De Havilland aircraft factory Eddie was sent by the Nazis to destroy.

✗

Reference: *Agent Zigzag* by Ben Macintyre.

✗

Peter James Quirk is an author, freelance writer and outdoorsman who spends his winters skiing and snowboarding and his summers hiking, biking and playing tennis. His novel *Trail of Vengeance* has a strong ski theme; indeed, the villain of the story is a disgraced ski instructor. Many of his stories, however, cover World War II and its aftermath. It is a fascinating if tragic period to explore, and the villains and heroes are so easy to find.

BROOKLYN'S ELUSIVE "MR. G":

BOOKIES AND COPS IN THE CITY OF CHURCHES

by Albert Ashforth

Sometimes the most ordinary actions trigger extraordinary events.

On a warm evening in September 1949, a guy felt thirsty after quitting work and decided to drop into a downtown Brooklyn tavern for a beer. The guy's name was Ed Reid, and he was a city-side reporter for the *Brooklyn Eagle* newspaper.

Next to Reid in the crowded bar were a bunch of characters talking about racing and betting, and the more they drank, the louder they talked. At one point one of the guys announced in no uncertain terms, "You can't do any bookmaking any more unless you're willing to work for Mr. G."

"Mr. G?" Reid asked himself. "Who's that?"

In looking for an answer to his own question, Reid triggered a series of events that erupted into the biggest police scandal in American history. The fallout from the scandal eventually caused the Mayor of New York City to submit his resignation, the Senate Committee on Organized Crime to visit New York to hold televised hearings, two grand juries to be empanelled to hear evidence of corruption—and ultimately brought about over 400 resignations and forced retirements among New York City's police and public servants.

And it all began with Ed Reid, beer in hand, wondering about the identity of "Mr. G."

After speaking with the *Eagle's* city editor about the pervasiveness of bookies and gambling in Brooklyn, Reid dropped into the office of Kings County District Attorney Miles F. McDonald and passed along what he had heard about "Mr. G."

Both McDonald and Reid were "old school" Brooklyn types. They believed laws should be obeyed and they understood the consequences of ordinary citizens openly flouting the rules and regulations that make life in a civilized society possible. They both felt that the citizens of Brooklyn, in closing their eyes to the corruption around them, were doing immense harm to themselves and their community.

"They mention Mr. G's full name?" McDonald asked.

Reid said they didn't, but the existence of a "Mr. G" jibed with some of the talk about a criminal mastermind that District Attorney McDonald and his investigators had also been hearing. Reid and McDonald knew, just as every other resident of Brooklyn knew, that it was as easy to get down a bet in "the city of churches" as it was to buy a pastrami sandwich. Anyone who took a minute to think about the situation found it baffling because of two circumstances: One, betting was illegal; and two, if the ordinary citizen knew where to place a bet, then so did the cop on the beat.

Reid and his city editor at the *Eagle* figured that the reason the police didn't arrest the bookmakers was because they were being paid to protect them. Reid began researching and in December 1949 the results of his investigation ran in the paper as an eight-part exposé on gambling in Brooklyn. Running under the headline "Lucrative Borough Rackets Feed Vast Crime Syndicate," the series described a criminal combine which ran "dope, prostitution, blackmail and other allied rackets"—but whose primary source of revenue was its Brooklyn gambling operation. With its lucrative bookmaking and policy rackets, Brooklyn was described as the heart and soul of a far-reaching criminal empire.

The series gave readers the impression bookies had pretty much taken over their borough and opened people's eyes to the tremendous amount of money being bet—on the horses, on sports like baseball and basketball, and on the numbers. Civic groups set up a clamor. For his part, McDonald reasoned that a certain amount of the gambling money was finding its way into the pockets of the city's police force.

In Reid's own words, the series "caused Brooklyn residents to react like startled deer." Until then, because of public indifference, the gambling situation and the police corruption it always engenders were a third rail for law enforcement authorities. But the unexpected public indignation caused by Reid's series led McDonald to believe that Brooklyn people might, at long last, be ready to support an attempt to clean up the corruption.

It was the District Attorney's investigation, which McDonald undertook against heavy opposition, that would eventually identify and ultimately topple "Mr. G"—and would set in motion events that would lead to the resignation of New York City's mayor.

Even before the newspaper publication of Reid's series, some people had a pretty good idea of how much money was being bet because they were taking a cut of the action.

Mayor William O'Dwyer probably wouldn't have been surprised to learn that the illegal betting handle in Brooklyn that year may have reached $20,000,000. A good portion of the illegal swag, about $1,200,000, was going either to the police in the form of bribes—or as the bookies call bribe money, "ice"—or into the pockets of O'Dwyer and his City Hall cronies. O'Dwyer and his people also knew something else—that the mysterious "Mr. G" had his gambling operation partially financed by a $100,000 loan from three highly-placed police officials, one of whom was an inspector and a close friend of the mayor.

O'Dwyer not only knew the identity of Brooklyn's "Mr. G," he knew that "Mr. G" was, for him, a ticking time bomb. Not only were some of the mayor's favorite political hacks on "Mr. G's" pad, many had been on it since 1946, the year O'Dwyer was elected mayor. One had been receiving "ice" from "Mr. G" since 1943, which was during the time O'Dwyer was still Brooklyn district attorney. When McDonald, who was O'Dwyer's successor as Brooklyn DA, began his investigation of illegal gambling and police corruption in January 1950, the mayor and his friends sensed that unless they could pressure the DA or sabotage the investigation, their days in City Hall were numbered.

But police corruption is hard to investigate because you can't use the police to do the investigating. In order to get around this roadblock, McDonald had Assistant District Attorney Julius Helfand recruit twenty-nine of the newest class of police academy graduates to go undercover. Helfand also set up a new chain of command, ensuring that the recruits reported directly to him and not to Commissioner William P. O'Brien, who was one of O'Dwyer's appointees. An even bigger problem for the Brooklyn DA: He had to work around not only O'Dwyer and Commissioner O'Brien but also such City Hall hacks as James J. Moran, the Deputy City Fire Commissioner, and August Flath, Chief Inspector of Police. Both were close associates of the mayor who always had their antennas tuned for any tidbit of news that might conceivably cause their boss problems.

After the appearance of Reid's stories on gambling, McDonald asked Judge Samuel Leibowitz, a legendary jurist who fifteen years before defended the Scottsboro Boys, to extend the session of the sitting Brooklyn grand jury. Then, during one of O'Dwyer's absences from the city, he asked the Board of Estimate for $60,000 to help finance the investigation. O'Dwyer responded by announcing to the newspapers that McDonald's investigation was "a witch hunt." In time, O'Dwyer's words and his numerous attempts to derail the investigation would come back to haunt him—but during the early months of 1950 New York City's citizens didn't know whom to believe.

Even editorial writers who should have known better paid the mayor's comments heed. When O'Dwyer, using an all-purpose put-down of those times, described McDonald's investigation as "Communist inspired," his sentiments were solemnly reported in all the city's papers.

O'Dwyer's many attempts to discredit McDonald had the effect not only of confusing people but also of stalling the investigation. As the DA's patched-together squad of rookies and honest police officers began rolling up the bookies and searching for the elusive "Mr. G," they were sometimes tricked into going on wild goose chases. On other occasions, word of impending raids and arrests was passed on to the racketeers and bookies. For McDonald and his assistants, Julius Helfand and Inspector Bill Dahut, it was at times extremely discouraging. It often seemed that half the city's civil servants were on "Mr. G's" payroll.

As a result, it wasn't until March 1950—some six months after Reid dropped into the Brooklyn bar—that the investigators were finally able to learn just who "Mr. G" actually was. The news came from an unexpected source and from out of the blue. A down-at-the-heels vagrant, after serving thirty days in jail, had become disenchanted with the life of a bookie's runner. It seems that the runner, whose name was Danny Fagin, felt his bookie boss had not just let him down; he'd used him as a fall guy in order to escape doing jail time himself. Out for revenge, Fagin called Ed Reid, who passed him along to Chief Inspector Dahut.

Fagin told Dahut his boss was a bookie named Jimmy Rossi, the owner of a downtown Brooklyn radio store. He said Rossi could have gotten him out of jail.

When Dahut asked why he thought Rossi could get him out of jail, Fagin said, "He works for Gross."

"Gross?" Dahut frowned, recalling that some time before, the police had arrested a Jack Gross ("Mr. G's" younger brother) and given him a suspended sentence. Dahut knew Fagin couldn't be talking about Jack, who was just a teenager and attending a local college.

Dahut asked Fagin which Gross he was talking about.

"Oh, Harry Gross," Fagin said helpfully. "They call him Mr. G. He's got connections with everybody. He coulda got me out of jail if Rossi asked him."

Once McDonald knew the identity of "Mr. G," his next job was to gather evidence and arrest him. Before he could do that, though, some bizarre events took place.

In July 1950, a Brooklyn police captain, shortly after testifying before a grand jury, shot himself in his own station house. By this time, seven months into McDonald's investigation, it was clear that no one could halt the momentum of events—not even, despite his best efforts to do so, Mayor William O'Dwyer. Publicly, though, O'Dwyer continued to blast the investigation and tried to pin the policeman's death on McDonald. He ordered all of the city's police to attend the captain's funeral, in uniform, with the result that some 6,000 police dutifully turned out.

O'Dwyer announced to reporters that District Attorney McDonald had "hounded" the policeman, who was innocent of any wrongdoing, to the point where he had taken his own life. It was a callous, calculated attempt by the mayor to exploit a tragic event for his own advantage.

Privately, O'Dwyer was planning his escape, not just from New York City politics but to a place beyond the authority of any district attorney's subpoena. Using all his political influence, he began frantically making calls and calling in favors.

O'Dwyer's connections extended into the White House and he was able to pull the right strings—which led to his legal difficulties coming to the attention of President Truman, who may or may not have had a clear picture of the extent of O'Dwyer's involvement with New York City's rackets. What is known is that, a little over a month later, on August 14, 1950, "Bill-O" suddenly announced that he would be resigning as Mayor of New York City and taking a post as Ambassador to Mexico. At the press conference, he avoided mentioning that, in answering his country's call to Mexico, he would be receiving $15,000 a year less in salary than he was receiving as mayor.

Many of O'Dwyer's cronies quickly concluded there was no preventing the inevitable and began looking for their own escape hatches. None of course would be able to come up with as elegant an exit as O'Dwyer's. Two of the mayor's closest friends, Inspector John E. Flynn and Chief of Detectives William T. Whalen, had no options beyond announcing their retirements. They were joined by flocks of detectives and police officers suddenly as eager to get off "the Job" as they had once been to get on it. Between April and November of 1950, 376 policemen were dismissed from the force, quit, or retired under a cloud.

Even after they identified him as "Mr. G," the police found Harry Gross elusive. Dahut and McDonald tracked Gross to the St. George Hotel on Clark Street in Brooklyn Heights, where he had a suite of rooms. But one of Gross's spies, an operator on the hotel switchboard, informed him that he was under police surveillance. Gross disappeared and the investigators found themselves back at square one.

A week went by before Dahut was again able to locate "Mr. G." Figuring Rossi's Fulton Street radio store was a major component of the gambling ring, Dahut staked out the place himself. One evening, he saw a man who looked like Harry Gross exit the store and climb into a large convertible. The car, as it turned out, was registered to none other than Harry Gross, a resident of Atlantic Beach, an area of posh homes just over the Queens line in Nassau.

This time, "Mr. G" did not get away.

✗   ✗   ✗   ✗

As a youngster growing up in Flatbush, I heard a great deal about Harry Gross.

When my mother, who had known him years before and used to encounter him from time to time, learned that he'd been arrested and charged with being the brains behind a vast gambling ring, she laughed. "Oh, Harry," she said and waved her hand dismissively. "No, no. It couldn't be Harry."

The truth was that Harry Gross just did not fit anyone's idea of a criminal mastermind—and this was one of the reasons he'd been able to fly comfortably under the radar for so long.

To start with, Harry Gross wasn't violent. In the criminal world of unpredictable psychopaths and violence-prone hoodlums, Harry never ordered a welsher to be beaten up. When it became obvious that one of his bookies was cheating him or holding out, Harry merely fired the dishonest employee. People liked doing business with Harry Gross, and people liked working for him.

Despite his easygoing façade, though, Harry Gross wasn't quite the laid-back individual some people took him to be. Even as a youngster, he possessed a combination of qualities that made him stand out from the other boys populating the teeming streets of the Flatbush section of Brooklyn. For one thing, he was totally self-centered. Harry always knew who was Number One and acted accordingly. Second, he loved money with a passion, and it was this love that supplied Harry's motivation and transformed him into a nearly unparalleled overachiever. Even though he could never spend a fraction of the money he earned, these vast sums were necessary to satisfy Harry's self-esteem and the needs of his outsized ego. And third, Harry possessed the qualities of an organizer and a natural leader.

But maybe most important, Harry Gross had a friendly charm and a winning smile.

As my mother, my sister and I walked up Flatbush Avenue, I could see a heavyset man in a gray suit dodging through the crowd and coming rapidly in our direction. When he saw us, he stopped.

"Hello, Mildred," he said, smiling. He had dark brown eyes beneath oval-shaped eyebrows and thick black hair.

"Hi, Harry. It's nice to see you."

"What beautiful children, Mildred. My goodness!"

"Say hello to Mr. Gross."

"Hello, Mr. Gross," we said in unison.

Seconds later, Harry Gross was on his way again, moving rapidly through the crowd of shoppers and strollers on the packed sidewalk.

It was hard not to like Harry. He never forgot a person's name and he seemingly had time for everyone. It is no wonder that people who knew Harry as a young man were never able to visualize him as a larger-than-life gangster or the mastermind behind a criminal empire whose tentacles reached not only into City Hall but all the way into the mayor's office.

Even as a young man Harry showed plenty of pluck and when he was fifteen, he concluded against the wishes of his parents that he'd had enough schooling. After graduating from P.S. 92 in Brooklyn, he decided it was time "to make a buck" and took a job as a soda jerk at Peller & Silverman's, a bustling drug store located on the southwest corner of Flatbush and Parkside Avenues. This was in the early 1930's at the very bottom of the Depression and times were hard. But the drug store had a prime location, just a few blocks south of Prospect Park on a prosperous stretch of Flatbush Avenue dotted with restaurants and movie palaces and not far from a nationally-known vaudeville theater. It was a section of expensive homes populated by families like the O'Malleys, who would later become owners of the Brooklyn baseball team. For Harry, it was a lively and diverting place to work. Skilled workers were being fired from their jobs, but working behind Peller & Silverman's soda fountain, scooping out ice cream and chatting up the customers, young Harry Gross flourished.

For Harry, jerking sodas was in many respects the ideal job—at least for a while. For one thing, Harry had a sweet tooth and the job gave him access to ice cream, which he ate in quantities. Throughout his life people would kid him about his weight and even when some of the soda fountain customers addressed him as "Pudgy" or "Fat Boy," he took the ribbing good-naturedly. Another advantage was that he got to wear a spiffy white soda jerk's uniform, which on Harry looked good and made him feel important. And of course many of Harry's customers were young women. Erasmus Hall High School, my mother's alma mater, was just three blocks away and beginning in mid-afternoon the coeds would drop in for ice cream sodas, banana splits, and frappes. With his gift for gab, disarming smile, and his willingness to add an extra scoop to a banana split, Harry had no trouble getting dates with some of the neighborhood's most attractive and intelligent young women.

Even though his parents were having difficulty making ends meet and Harry's father eventually lost his laundry business, Harry maintained his own comfortable lifestyle, taking out girls, going to the movies, and buying clothes. While still a teenager, he began spending money in other ways. After work, he visited pool halls and, like a lot of other people in Brooklyn in those years, developed an interest in gambling. At first, it was cards and dice. Later, with horses like War Admiral, Whirlaway, and Seabiscuit capturing the public's imagination, Harry became an obsessive horseplayer. Although the term had not been coined in the 1930's, Harry Gross, hardly out of his teens, already exhibited the qualities of a "degenerate gambler," and would remain one throughout his life. Deep within, he had the urge to show everyone that he was smarter than they were—and for him the way to prove that was to outsmart them by winning their money. Harry Gross's ego was close to insatiable and in the course of his life it would lead him to do some strange things.

Ultimately, it was his uncontrollable passion for gambling that would determine not only the course of Harry Gross's life but, tragically, the course of quite a few other people's lives as well.

Where gambling was concerned, Harry started small, taking bets at the soda fountain for a neighborhood bookie. He was very smooth—getting down names and numbers, quoting odds, collecting, and paying off winners so unobtrusively the owners of the drug store only tumbled to Harry's "sideline" when some of the other neighborhood bookies complained. Harry, they said, was moving into what they considered to be their "territory." When he was fired, Harry exhibited the same decisiveness and self-confidence he would show during later crises in his life.

He immediately got another job.

Continuing as a soda jerk, Harry went to work at another drug store, Reid and Yeoman's, which was located at the corner of Flatbush Avenue and Cortelyou Road, only a few blocks away from his previous employer. Although my mother described this corner as less prosperous than the Parkside Avenue location, it was in some ways better because it was busier, a transportation and business hub. But right next door to the drug store was a barbershop and across Cortelyou Road was a bar, and another bookie operated in plain sight on the corner.

As my mother waited at Reid and Yeoman's prescription counter, my four-year-old-sister toddled off in the direction of the soda fountain, curiously eyeing the customers seated on high stools downing their sundaes and ice cream sodas. To her surprise, she saw that the soda jerk with a broad smile on his face was motioning to her. He wanted her to come down to the end of the counter where she could climb onto a stool and he could hand her the vanilla ice cream cone which he was holding in his hand.

But after my sister had clambered up onto the stool, my mother intervened. "Harry, I didn't ask—"

Still smiling, Harry Gross insisted on presenting my sister with the ice cream cone. "It's fine, Mildred."

"I have to pay you, Harry," my mother said, frantically fishing around in her pocketbook for some change. But Harry was already on his way to the far end of the counter to serve another customer.

Back at the prescription counter and eating her ice cream, my sister couldn't understand my mother's irritation, which was caused by always wanting to pay for anything she received. But as Harry knew, five cents was more money than she could often afford to spend for ice cream.

As they left the drugstore, my mother, much calmer now, told my sister, "Wave goodbye to Mr. Gross."

When Harry began taking bets at the new soda fountain, the other bookies in the barbershop and in the bar became miffed. The truth was, Harry with his ingratiating manner and warm smile was making big inroads into his competitors' business. People liked to do business with Harry. Eventually, Harry was fired from Reid and Yeoman's, again for taking bets on the job. He then went to work at a newly opened luncheonette on the other side of Flatbush Avenue.

But as he learned the bookie business, Harry saw he could function more effectively by moving around and visiting bettors than by manning one post all day. Harry left the luncheonette and began circulating through the neighborhood. Dodging the big red trolley cars that clanged and rumbled and, as I remember, seemed to come at you from all directions, Harry covered Flatbush Avenue from Empire Boulevard to Dorchester Road. He visited the gin mills, groceries, candy stores, barber shops, restaurants, and drug stores, currying favor with proprietors and customers alike with his aggressive but friendly manner. Some bettors he would meet right on the street. Recalling this time in his life, Harry later said, "When I would see people, I would tell them I wanted some business and I would appreciate it if they would give it to me." Many did, and it is easy to see why. Win or lose, people found Harry to be a friendly, ingratiating Brooklyn guy, fun to talk with, easy to do business with, definitely one of their own.

As Harry himself described those days, "I did very good."

But there were problems. As an independent bookie working the streets of Brooklyn in the early 1940's, Harry was vulnerable—and he was often arrested. It took a while, but he finally got smart. As he later told the court, one day in the summer of 1941 he was on Church Avenue and talking with a bettor when a plainclothesman grabbed him.

After a brief argument about whether or not Harry was taking bets, the cop finally said, "You're a sucker for working this way. You ought to get an O.K." When Harry asked what an "O.K." was and how he could get one, the cop said he'd check things out.

Harry finally figured it out: to be successful in the bookie business, you needed to buy police protection. As in every other business, you needed to spend money to make money. When the policeman returned, he gave Harry the lowdown on how much "ice" he had to pay to keep from being arrested and harassed by the police. Even Harry was surprised by the size of the payoffs the cops were demanding.

The extent of Harry Gross's earnings in the early-1940's can be guessed at from the fact that he was soon doling out $800 every month for police protection. Later on, he would pay much more. During these years, Harry held court late Saturday night in Oetjen's, a fashionable restaurant on Church Avenue, paying the "ice" and shooting the breeze with whichever cops came around to collect. For policemen getting off the four-to-twelve, Oetjen's, with "Knuckles" O'Craven at the piano, was the ideal place to go to unwind and wrap up the week. And it was made better by the fact that at the end of the evening, Harry paid everyone's tab.

At about this time, Harry opened his first horse room. He rented a garage just a block from Brooklyn's oldest landmark, the Dutch Reformed Church, had it painted and fitted it out with some chairs and tables, scratch sheets, and copies of the *Morning Telegraph*. It had a telephone, but Harry still didn't have the know-how to rent a Western Union racing ticker, which was always a fixture in the best horse rooms in Manhattan. But the chances are that Harry's Church Avenue clientele weren't all that demanding and were content to bet only the races at the local tracks.

Except for a miserable four months that he spent in the United States Army in 1942 and some betting miscalculations he made in 1948 and 1949, the 1940's were a good decade for Harry Gross. In 1946, he got married and moved with his wife into a house in the Sheepshead Bay section of Brooklyn. After the birth of his two children, he bought a larger and more expensive home in Atlantic Beach. As Ed Reid learned in the downtown bar, by 1949 "Mr. G" had the gambling business pretty much sewed up and all the bookies in Brooklyn working for him. Besides his Brooklyn operation, Harry had horse rooms in three other boroughs as well.

All kinds of circumstances in those years seemed to be conspiring to encourage Brooklyn people to want to wager.

With the Dodgers in the pennant race nearly every year, fans wanted to do more than just cheer for Robinson and Reese and company at Ebbets Field—with the result that there was a dramatic increase in the amount of money being bet on baseball. The Friday night fights at Madison Square Garden became the focus of national attention and increased betting action on boxing. With money from his gambling enterprise, Harry bought into a number of Brooklyn restaurants and nightclubs. In the early 1940's, at a time when highly skilled workers were bringing home salaries of less than $5,000—and most policemen were earning less than $3,000—Harry Gross was earning $75,000 a year. Considering his modest Brooklyn lifestyle, you would think that would have been more than Harry could ever hope to spend.

But he succeeded in spending it, anyway. In 1948, he gambled away all the money he had stashed. Believing that President Truman didn't have a chance of winning the 1948 presidential election, Harry bet on Thomas E. Dewey, then the Governor of New York State—and lost a bundle. What most bothered Harry, though, was the thought that losing so much money made him look dumb. The famous gambler "Jimmy the Greek" Snyder, for example, not only made a killing when he bet on President Truman, he established a reputation for being able to pick long-shot winners, which he used as a springboard to comparative respectability. For a time, he was even a sports commentator on a TV network.

While people were looking up to Jimmy, they were laughing at Harry. In order to remain Brooklyn's boss bookie, Harry didn't need so much to recoup his money as to regain his now tarnished reputation. But as in the past, the demands of Harry's ego began to drive him to extremes. Maybe his many clients couldn't solve the intricacies of the sport of kings, but Harry knew he was smarter than they were. Believing he could beat the odds, Harry began plunging, betting with the ring controlled by one of the country's most notorious bookies, Frank Erickson, a pal of Frank Costello's—a mobster known for tying concrete blocks to the feet of welshers before dropping them into New York Harbor.

In the fall of 1949, less than a year after the 1948 election, Harry made some more colossal miscalculations, these having to do with horses. It was at this time that the qualities of a "degenerate" horseplayer kicked in. Each time he would lose, Harry, in an effort to get back to "even," would increase the size of his wager. As he doubled and tripled the size of his bets, Harry continued to lose, and eventually went broke. To make matters worse, he had gone into debt with some shylocks not noted for their patience with slow payers. Eventually, Harry owed Erickson and the moneylenders over $100,000 and didn't have the money to pay.

Worried by stories of the fate of welshers, he decided to take a powder. He went out to Newark Airport and boarded a flight to California.

Among the people who liked Harry and found him a dependable guy to do business with were some highly-placed officials in the Police Department. Three of them, one of them an inspector, raised $100,000 and bailed Harry out of his predicament by lending him the money to pay off Erickson. The deal was arranged by Harry's partner in the bookie operation, a well-connected former plainclothesman named James E. Reardon, nicknamed "the Connecticut Squire." Reardon, who had a greater interest in playing golf than in catching crooks, quit "the Job" some years earlier when Harry made him an offer the NYPD could never hope to match. Harry returned to New York, resumed his position as Brooklyn's boss bookie and paid off the loan in a matter of months.

It may have been in his many conversations with Jimmy Reardon that Harry grasped the real secret to running a successful gambling operation—which was not just to buy off the police, but to make them feel grateful to you and imagine themselves to be in your debt. Although it's probably fair to say that no one, before or since, has ever lavished money on the police of any city like Harry Gross did, it was the manner in which Gross paid his "ice" that brought the police under his control.

There's no group of people anywhere tougher or more cynical than New York City's cops. It's a measure of Harry Gross's own smarts that, in time, he had so many of them eating out of his hand.

Not content just to pay a cop as you might a business partner, Harry would cement relationships by making them personal. When Harry Gross turned on his charm, people believed he truly liked them, and found it hard to credit that he only wanted something from them in return. Going back to his soda fountain days, Harry first developed his approach when dealing with customers, then refined it when he realized he wanted something more than a smile from the attractive young women who streamed into the drug store for ice cream sodas and frappes. Later, in dealing with bettors on the streets, Harry refined his approach still further, telling people quite honestly that he wanted their business. By the time he began dealing with the police, Harry had it down to a science. Cops found it hard to believe that Harry was throwing parties for them and giving them presents only because he wanted them to overlook their responsibilities—and not because he cared about them as people. But the truth was that Harry Gross, then as always, cared for no one but himself.

Harry expended much time and effort getting to know policemen personally, giving intimate parties at expensive hotels where he would talk to them about their families, their neighborhoods, their problems. If a policeman needed money, Harry would lend it and not expect to be repaid. Another practice was to have a gift like a TV set delivered to a policeman's home. Of course, this meant there was a record of a policeman having received a present from Harry, an invisible sword of Damocles hanging over the officer's head. Harry learned women's sizes, and showered cops' wives with clothing, jewelry, and accessories. When he moved into his Brooklyn home, he threw an extravagant housewarming to which he invited dozens of cops. He attended graduations and remembered policemen's children with gifts at their first communion. He was particularly generous around Christmas, thoughtfully providing expensive toys for youngsters whose cop fathers he knew might have difficulty just managing the price of a Christmas tree.

Policemen did not just like Harry Gross, they romanticized him. For them, he was a "Robin Hood," someone who was taking money from the racketeers who normally profited from illegal gambling and returning it to the underpaid working people of the borough—and ultimately making Brooklyn a better place to live. For many cops the "ice" made it possible to meet mortgage payments. Cops' families, who otherwise might have been squeezed into squalid little apartments, were living in houses on tree-shaded streets. Parents were able to afford tuition payments at colleges—with the result that any number of cops' kids who otherwise never would have had the chance to see the inside of a college classroom, became lawyers, doctors, and teachers. Cops were taking their families on Sunday drives in cars that, if it weren't for Harry Gross, they never would have owned. Later, stories would surface of policemen not just protecting Harry from the law, but from competition from bookies who wanted to move in on Harry's business.

The relationship that existed between Harry Gross and the borough's police could only have existed in a tightly knit community of working people protective of their families and fiercely loyal to one another—in other words, only in Brooklyn.

It was the nature of this relationship that ultimately caused the downfall of so many policemen —and led, tragically, to the biggest police scandal in the history of the United States. If not completely innocent, many of the policemen were naïve, failing to realize as they accepted presents from a bookie, how they were becoming tangled up in his illegal business and becoming his accomplices in ruining the lives of compulsive gamblers. Cops who would never have considered taking graft from a prostitute or a drug dealer listened to Harry—and let themselves be persuaded that betting was a harmless pastime, not an evil one. Even as a youngster on the sidewalks of Flatbush, Harry had been more cunning than the other boys. As an adult, he was still far ahead of the pack.

When Harry Gross finally went down, he took an enormous number of people with him.

Detectives from District Attorney Miles McDonald's squad arrested Harry Gross in his two-room suite at the Towers Hotel in Brooklyn Heights on September 15, 1950, just one year after Ed Reid dropped into the downtown Brooklyn bar for a beer.

By this time, the police had been on Gross's tail for days, staking out his haunts, ID'ing his accomplices, and tapping his phones. As a result of raids on his telephone operation and accounting office, McDonald had names, telephone numbers, and the addresses of Gross's horse rooms all over the city. But even McDonald, as he became familiar with Gross's operation, was astounded by the amount of money the business brought in—maybe as much as $50,000 per day. To keep things going, Gross commanded a well-drilled team of bookies, runners, telephone operators, and horse room people. On his payroll he had a number of salaried accountants to keep accurate records of the financial end of his business. The net annual profit of "Mr. G's" gambling operation, according to Walter Arm, who covered Gross's arrest for the *New York Herald-Tribune*, was in the neighborhood of $2,000,000—although, in hindsight, that figure seems high. According to Arm, the "ice" earmarked just for the upper echelons of the Police Department could have been close to $500,000.

These were the people who were the main target of McDonald's investigation: the policemen and City Hall politicians who had taken bribes in exchange for providing protection. Not surprisingly, Harry was his usual affable and loquacious self in the first hours after his arrest, laughingly observing, "There'll be a lot of worried people in the city tonight." Maybe William O'Dwyer, now on his way to Mexico, didn't have to worry—but many of his City Hall friends did. In time, people would see this remark as a colossal understatement.

Gross talked non-stop, but balked whenever he was asked to name the cops on his payroll. Speaking to Judge Samuel Leibowitz, he nobly announced he was torn between his desire to tell the truth and his loyalty to the many policemen he had befriended over the years. Many policemen still regarded Harry not only as a friend but as a kind of Robin Hood, unfortunately now in the clutches of the

Sheriff of Nottingham. Needless to say, neither Judge Leibowitz nor DA McDonald saw many Robin Hood-like qualities in Harry Gross, whom they regarded only as a very slick con man—and they sensed that in dealing with him they would have to be careful.

Remembering the fate that befell Abe Reles, who had been a material witness against Murder Inc. and had "fallen" out of a hotel window while O'Dwyer was Brooklyn District Attorney, McDonald didn't want Harry Gross back on the street. In order to make sure Gross would remain safely behind bars, he charged him not with bookmaking but as a material witness, which made it possible to ask that Gross be held in lieu of $250,000 cash bail. Gross thought he'd be out of police clutches within a couple of days, but that kind of bail was more money than even he could raise. Brooklyn's Raymond Street jail, to which Gross was remanded, was a rat-filled ancient building, and the guards there felt no necessity to bow and scrape to "Mr. G." The police figured Gross would quickly crack. In order to keep the pressure on, Judge Leibowitz ordered that Gross be kept apart from the other prisoners and given a cell with a bright light that burned around the clock.

"He can't take jail," Bill Dahut told McDonald. "In a couple of weeks he'll be begging for help."

✗   ✗   ✗   ✗

It was the beginning of a war of nerves between Gross and DA McDonald, with hundreds of policemen as nervous onlookers.

It's easy to see why policemen like Bill Dahut thought Gross couldn't take an extended jail term. Harry Gross gave every appearance of a guy who enjoyed all the perquisites of a successful racketeer—carrying a gigantic roll of bills with him at all times, wearing expensive clothes, eating well, and being chauffeured around in a Cadillac. Because he seemed good-natured, he was a very easy person to underestimate, and probably his success depended, to some extent, on people underestimating him. He looked soft, like someone who did very little physical exercise. Always on the chunky side, he was still overweight from too much ice cream and cheesecake. He spoke with a Brooklyn accent, often ungrammatically, and at times didn't seem all that bright.

In reality he was as cagey as ever and he recognized he was in a battle of wits with a tough, smart district attorney. Although McDonald had surprised Gross by seeking and getting high bail, you don't get to be the "boss bookie" by lying down and playing dead the minute things don't go your way. Harry still had a few cards to play.

My mother, who closely followed Gross's trial for bookmaking and conspiracy, was surprised when Harry pleaded guilty and received a twelve-year sentence. Like a lot of people who knew him personally but had no first-hand knowledge of his gambling operation, she wondered whether he deserved such a long jail term. As a young man at the soda fountain, he'd always been engaging, thoughtful, and full of fun.

In April 1951, after seven months in jail, Gross threw in the towel—or at least pretended to. He announced that in return for a reduced sentence of four years, he was willing to identify bribe-takers by name and true to his word, he went before a Grand Jury where he did a lot of talking—providing much information on how the police protected the bookies. Among the names Gross mentioned was that of Police Commissioner William P. O'Brien. According to Gross, he began paying "ice" to O'Brien eight years earlier in 1943, when O'Brien was an inspector in the 19th Division. For each horse room within the 19th's jurisdiction, Gross said, he paid O'Brien $200 each week. It is probably not a coincidence that O'Brien retired just ten days after Gross's arrest.

As a result of his testimony, seventy-seven officers were indicted for conspiracy to obstruct justice. Eventually, on September 10, 1951, eighteen policemen—including one inspector, one captain, and two lieutenants—were brought to trial. As the prosecutor pointed out as the trial began, a gambling operation of such magnitude could not have existed without protection and cooperation from the police at all levels "right up to the police commissioner's office." Despite the massive amount of evidence of widespread police corruption, however, the case against the defendants—who, among them, had seventy children—rested entirely on the testimony of Harry Gross.

Perhaps because of the way he blew hot one day and cold the next, prosecutors wanted to keep their high-strung witness relaxed and happy. On the second day of the trial, McDonald gave Gross permission to visit his family in their Long Island home. But as it happened, there were still people around who would fall victim to Harry's line of baloney and, unfortunately, two of them were the young police officers with the job of guarding him that afternoon. Harry was all wisecracks and jokes as they rode out to Long Island. When the cops left Gross unguarded for a few minutes, he slipped out the back door, jumped into his car, and disappeared.

He was only gone for a day and a half.

Late the next afternoon, a state trooper on duty at an Atlantic City racetrack spotted someone who looked like Harry standing in line at the $50 betting window.

"Pardon me," he said, "but aren't you Harry Gross?"

The man said he was.

Gross wanted to be found. He probably breathed a large sigh of relief when he was recognized. If certain members of the New York City Police Department or particular denizens of the Brooklyn underworld had been first to locate him, the story might have had a different ending.

Why had he taken off? Back in Brooklyn, Harry said innocently, "I just wanted to get away. Anything the matter with that?"

Harry was ready to play another card, but no one knew it yet.

When the trial resumed, Harry Gross, as chipper as ever, returned to the witness stand, at first recalling his early years in Flatbush and how he started as a bookie. For a while, everything went smoothly. But when Assistant District Attorney Helfand asked him to give the names of policemen he had bribed, he clammed up. Gross's sudden refusal to name names turned the courtroom into, as the *Brooklyn Eagle* described it, "a scene of wild confusion never before witnessed in a local court." The cops couldn't believe their good fortune and started laughing and cheering. Without Gross's testimony, the case against them would have to be dismissed. Because of the law against double jeopardy, they couldn't be retried. Robin Hood had again outsmarted the Sheriff of Nottingham.

Gross suddenly bolted from the courtroom but returned a few minutes later. He said he was suffering from an "upset stomach." When Judge Leibowitz asked if he was willing to return the following day, he said he would.

But when he took the stand on September 19, Gross announced, "I won't answer any questions."

Aware that Gross had tried to make him look foolish, Judge Leibowitz became furious. He charged Gross with sixty contempt citations, then threatened to give him "life."

Like DA McDonald and Ed Reid, Judge Leibowitz saw Harry Gross in a different light than did the indicted policemen. Pointing toward Gross, he said, "This man has stabbed, has put a dagger through the hearts of the people of New York. No man... has done more to harm law and order than he has." Because of Gross's close friendship with so many police officers and their families, there was a good deal of truth in Leibowitz's statements. It is hard to think of anyone who wreaked more havoc in the lives of so many people as Harry Gross.

"Why don't you give me the chair and get it over with?" Gross said to Leibowitz, very much in the style of Robin Hood taunting the Sheriff of Nottingham.

Judge Leibowitz didn't give Gross the chair, but he sentenced him to serve thirty days on each of the contempt charges. He also reinstated Gross's original sentence of twelve years, eight more years than McDonald agreed he should serve as a result of his guilty plea and in recognition of his grand jury testimony. Harry Gross was on his way back to jail, but he had the satisfaction of knowing he'd put one over on the DA, the cops, and Judge Leibowitz, whom Gross didn't like personally. Even if he didn't qualify as Robin Hood, that was pretty good for a former soda jerk from Flatbush who'd spent years taking bets on Flatbush Avenue while dodging trolley cars and who quit school after the 8th grade. At least that's what he may have thought at the time.

Gross's refusal to testify meant that two years of work by District Attorney McDonald, the police recruits, and the DA's squad, gathering evidence and making a case, had been in vain. It was definitely a blow to the district attorney and the honest cops who'd been on the trail of "Mr. G" for close to two years.

By this time there were any number of people around who wished they'd never heard the name Harry Gross. One of them was James E. Reardon, the former plainclothesman who, after six years as a policeman, quit the department in 1946 to become a partner with Gross. Reardon felt Gross let his friends, his co-workers, and the policemen down when he testified before the Grand Jury and at the police department trials. Reardon eventually served three and-a-half years for perjury in connection with his own Grand Jury testimony.

Another might have been James J. Moran, who according to Gross, asked him to contribute to what he called a "bookies' fund" to help get O'Dwyer elected mayor. Frank Costello was one of O'Dwyer's chief financial backers in those years, and this meant Harry Gross was another. After being convicted of perjury for lying to the Senate Committee investigating organized crime, Moran was convicted of extortion in a trial at which he was defended by George Wolf, the same lawyer who often defended Frank Costello. All told, Moran served nearly twelve years in prison. As O'Dwyer's bag man, he'd handled millions of dollars in graft, bribes, and ice, and the government estimated his 1949-50 income at $297, 960—but he died from a heart attack in 1966 while riding the New York City subway.

Moran stayed loyal to O'Dwyer even while his old boss was hosting parties at the American Embassy and soaking up the Mexican sunshine. As Brooklyn's District Attorney during the early 1940's, O'Dwyer would have known of Gross's weekly "ice" sessions at Oetjen's Restaurant and of some of the more prominent Brooklyn horse rooms, one of which was in the cozy backyard of the Dugout Restaurant on Empire Boulevard, not far from Ebbets Field. It's likely that in 1945 O'Dwyer personally sent Moran to collect from Gross to support his first mayoral campaign. The former mayor of the world's greatest city, fearful of the subpoenas and indictments that awaited him in the United States, eventually became a permanent resident of Mexico. He didn't return to New York until shortly before his death from a heart attack in 1964.

According to Assistant District Attorney Helfand, Gross's sudden refusal to testify at the trial was "planned and concocted." When the smoke cleared, it became obvious that Gross, in escaping for a day, had done more than visit a racetrack. Gross never revealed where he went or with whom he spoke on his one day of freedom, but it is believed he met with a group of mobsters at a house in Newark. Judge Leibowitz believed that Gross had been coached regarding his conduct at the trial by a "legal architect" who mapped out a legal strategy more sophisticated than anything

Gross alone could have devised. It was rumored that for his refusal to testify, the mob paid him $60,000, not much for a guy who had been earning millions. It's more likely that Gross feared being killed if he testified against the policemen.

After Gross played his trump, it was McDonald's turn to play his.

Without Gross's testimony, bribe-taking police officers could not be charged as criminals, but they could be charged for dereliction of duty at departmental trials. After another eight months in jail, Gross again changed his mind. Although he still refused to testify against the policeman in court, he testified at three department trials, at which more than fifty officers were found guilty of taking graft. By this time, the number of officers who left the force because of their involvement with Gross was over 400. Because of this limited cooperation, McDonald agreed for a second time to reduce Gross's sentence, this time from twelve to eight years.

Harry Gross served seven-and-a-half years and was released from jail in March 1958. The Brooklyn to which he briefly returned was much changed. The *Brooklyn Eagle*, the newspaper for which Ed Reid worked and which covered Gross's trials with banner headlines, ceased publication in January 1955. The Brooklyn Dodger baseball team played its last game in Brooklyn on September 24 of the previous year, and the club was on its way to California. Ebbets Field, where Gross used to enjoy hanging out while taking in night games, was waiting to be demolished. Even the garage on Church Avenue where Gross established his first horse room had been remodeled, and was now a small office building.

While still in jail, Harry Gross began a relationship with a Brooklyn dress shop owner, who said he'd promised to marry her and later filed a complaint that he'd bilked her out of $13,800. This was the first of the many legal problems which would haunt Gross for the remainder of his life.

The Harry Gross who emerged from prison was an entirely different individual from the low-profile and genial "Mr. G" who ran the Brooklyn bookmaking operation for so many years. Jail changed Gross, transforming him into a violence-prone petty gangster brimming over with hostility and a dislike for authority of any kind. After his release, he moved to the West Coast, where his wife and two children were already living. But in July 1959, just sixteen months after he had left jail, Los Angeles police arrested Gross for shooting and killing his wife's eighty-four-year-old grandfather in an argument over a gambling debt. In October of that year, he pleaded guilty to manslaughter and received a six-month-to-ten-year prison term.

It comes as no surprise that the following year Lila Gross, after a long estrangement, finally divorced Harry. Gross served three years of his manslaughter sentence and was released on parole in October 1962, but in February 1963 he was re-arrested for a parole violation and returned to prison. After again being released, he was arrested for drunk driving. In December 1966 he again violated parole and was sent back to prison.

By this time, Gross was an embittered man, someone who believed he'd been unfairly singled out by law enforcement authorities and punished excessively for the crimes he'd committed. In fact it's doubtful that he ever believed betting and bookmaking were really crimes—and he was often heard complaining about the hypocrisy of allowing betting at race tracks, but prohibiting it elsewhere. He now seemed to be incapable of leading a life other than that of a small-time career criminal, a life much different from the one he led as Brooklyn's "boss bookie"—when he regularly dined at New York City's best restaurants, wore custom-made clothing, and made his rounds in a chauffeured Cadillac. Despite numerous attempts to organize West Coast bookmaking operations, Gross was never able to climb back to the top—or even come anywhere close.

In August 1972 he was arrested for being in receipt of stolen property and for securities violations, but the charges were later dropped. In February 1974, he was again charged with receiving stolen property, but on this occasion was found guilty. He was given a five-year sentence at the Federal Corrections Institution at San Pedro, California. After his release, Gross was arrested a number of times for gambling. In February 1981 he was again sent to prison, this time for conspiracy to organize a bookmaking operation, and served two years.

Gross spent the last thirty years of his life 3,000 miles from Brooklyn, in southern California, much of that time behind bars. He never revisited the crowded Brooklyn streets where, as the untouchable "Mr. G," he'd built up his million-dollar bookie business, regularly rubbed shoulders with some of New York City's most prominent public officials—and tangled up the lives of so many Brooklyn people, many of whom had regarded Gross as a friend. It's anybody's guess how much he thought about the thousands of people whose lives he'd helped ruin, of the suicides, emotional collapses, and divorces that followed from his conviction and subsequent Grand Jury testimony—or of the stinging rebuke of Judge Leibowitz that he had "put a dagger through the hearts of the people of New York."

In March 1986, Harry Gross was arrested in Los Angeles by Federal Drug Enforcement agents. Living alone in a small Long Beach apartment, he was still haunted by memories of the Brooklyn years. Facing indictment for heroin trafficking, Harry Gross spiraled down into depression and decided he had nothing more to live for. On April 1, 1986 he was found in his apartment in a pool of blood with his wrists slashed. He left a note saying he'd decided that killing himself was preferable to "going back to prison and dying there." In the apartment was a flight bag containing $100,000 in bills, which agents said was payment for thirteen pounds of heroin which he sold to an accomplice in a drug ring.

Harry Gross died pretty much as he lived—with a suitcase full of money at his side, a felony conviction hanging over his head, and a jail term staring him in the face.

NOTE

Because of its many houses of worship, Brooklyn has been widely known as "the city of churches," ever since its incorporation as a city in the 1830's. Although you don't hear the sobriquet quite as often today, the title of a recent award-winning TV series was "Brooklyn: City of Churches."

Gross's downfall was tragic. As a young guy, he was intelligent, energetic, and thoughtful, and probably could have succeeded at whatever he tried. But he loved the horses. And he was right. The gambling laws, which allowed betting at the tracks but nowhere else, were hypocritical. Jail changed him, made him violent and bitter. After getting out, he was a wanted man in Brooklyn for giving up the cops' names. He had to go out to the Coast. His partner Jimmy Reardon wouldn't talk with him. Reardon's son owns the

Hudson Yards Cafe on 10th Avenue and I used to stop by now and then and shoot the breeze.

Joe Ponzi, on the Brooklyn DA's squad, told me how his father, also a policeman, talked about Gross all the time. Gross and a few pals had boxes at Ebbets Field behind third base. Leo Durocher used to say hello to them before the games, before he was suspended from baseball in 1947 for consorting with gamblers.

Gross's last years in California were sad. The newspapers hardly mentioned his death. People had forgotten his impact. Mayor O'Dwyer was on Gross's pad and needed President Truman to rescue him. Over 400 policemen were forced into retirement.

It was next to impossible to have lived in Flatbush during the 1940's and '50's without hearing about Harry Gross or having your life touched by him in one way or another. As I mention, my mother knew Harry Gross personally, and the fact that she recalled him so vividly is an indication that Harry had a memorable personality.

As a member of Western Union's cable gang, my father installed and maintained Western Union's cables, including the racing wire, for whichever customers wanted the service. In the late 1940's, Gross probably controlled in the neighborhood of thirty horse rooms, and although nothing bored my father more than sports and betting, he knew all of the horse rooms in New York City at first hand. Even though betting on the races was illegal in New York, he didn't feel it was Western Union's job to concern itself with what went out over its racing wire, any more than it is AT&T's job to monitor whatever goes out over any of its lines.

I want to express particular thanks to Brooklyn District Attorney Charles J. Hynes and Chief Investigator Joseph Ponzi for their invaluable help with this article and also for their tremendous patience in answering my questions. They provided me with much information that I could not have found elsewhere.

In filling out Harry Gross's story, I leaned heavily on contemporary news stories contained in the pages of the Brooklyn Eagle and the New York Times. The following books contain significant information about Harry Gross's career, mostly up until when he was convicted and sent away, and on the gambling situation generally. They were all immensely helpful in completing the picture I had of Harry Gross.

✗   ✗   ✗   ✗

Arm, Walter. *Payoff: The Inside Story of Big City Corruption*. New York: Appleton-Century-Crofts, 1951.

Cook, Fred J. *A Two-Dollar Bet Means Murder.* Westport: Greenwood Press, 1972.

Mockridge, Norton and Robert H. Prall. *The Big Fix*. New York: Henry Holt and Company, 1954.

Reid, Ed. *The Shame of New York.* New York: Random House, 1953.

Sasuly, Richard. *Bookies and Bettors*. New York: Holt. Rinehart & Winston, 1982.

Walsh, George. *Public Enemies.* New York: Norton, 1980.

✗

After serving with the U.S. Army overseas, Albert Ashforth received a degree from Brooklyn College and subsequently worked on two New York City newspapers. As a military contractor, Mr. Ashforth has done tours in Bosnia, Germany, Kosovo, Macedonia and Afghanistan. Mr. Ashforth has written three books and numerous stories, articles and reviews on a variety of subjects. His articles have been published in *American Scholar*, the *New York Times Magazine*, *Four Seasons*, the *Mystery Writers Annual* and other publications. His novel *The Rendition* was described by *Publishers Weekly* as "an exciting spy thriller" and was awarded the bronze medal from the Military Writers Society of America as one of the three best thrillers of 2012. *The Rendition* was recently a Kindle #1 selection in the Historical Thrillers category. Mr. Ashforth lives in New York City.

RED JACKS WILD

by Kim Newman

I'm John Carmody but… yes, you can call me Jack.

As it happens, I didn't come up with the "trade-name." Those letters weren't from me. I daresay a reporter needed to fill column inches. With no fresh kills, interest dies down. I'd have obliged the gentlemen of the press, but the ritual precludes indiscriminate slaughter. So, an unknown hack dashed off red-ink scrawls signed "yours truly, Jack the Ripper." The catchy tag got the story back on the front page.

I'm an American, though I studied surgery—and other, more arcane disciplines—in London. I am a qualified medical doctor, devout in my religion and a licensed psychoanalyst. Stretching on the couch in my office on West 74th Street and telling me your dreams sets you back seventy-five dollars an hour. Plus tax, old man…

The consulting work I do for the FBI and the NYPD is pro bono. It helps me keep abreast of developments in my field. Also, listening to manic ad execs and depressive wives get boring. Criminal analysis is a mental tonic. Seeking out like minds keeps mine sharp.

In 1951, I celebrated my 100th birthday yet I look no older than I did in 1888. The secret of my success is… well, killing disposable people.

Suffice to say, I've kept my bargain with Hecate. A ritual, repeated every third fall. Six offerings. Six bodies, arranged *just so*… to propitiate the Goddess of the Moon.

No, it doesn't get easier…

When I sacrificed on the altars of Whitechapel, the brightest sparks in criminology thought a crook was identifiable by the bumps on his head. No one knew about fingerprints. A policeman couldn't ask impertinent questions of a social superior. It was a miracle if any half-intelligent wrong 'un got caught.

In '51, the ritual was dicier. If the FBI hadn't called me in to work up a dossier—they call them profiles, now—I might not have completed it.

It helps to select your disposables carefully. Certain victims command fewer police resources than, say, archdukes or bankers' wives. As the world knows, I began on whores. Still a good wheeze. I fall back on street sluts whenever nothing else came to mind. In New Orleans in 1909, I took colored children. They called me the Voo-Doo Man. The cops didn't listen to the parents until I was done. In California in 1933, as the Hobo Hacker, I picked on jobless transients.

Last time, the Red Knife preyed on card-carrying communists... labor organisers, blacklisted teachers, a writer, an actress. I left their cards inside their open stomachs. Some commentators half-seriously said the killings might not technically be a crime. Other Red Knives were inspired to action, which made it easy to pin my offerings on a patsy. I spun a lot of analytical moonshine and led Special Agents Finlay and Dwight to Abner Polk. Expelled from a back-room revolutionary cell, Polk had dismembered two comrades. I walked the boob—sozzled on hooch and gore—through a confession. He wound up taking credit for six additional murders.

Public sympathy for the Red Knife evaporated. Polk wasn't a True American, but another Killer Commie, as bad as his victims. I had a ticket to his execution at Sing-Sing. They gave him more juice than the Rosenbergs.

Once, the world was satisfied with an unsolved mystery... the ship that vanished... the killer who was never caught... the unknown monster in the fog. Now, the public want a final chapter of the serial, an explanation for the magic, and a villain to strap into the electric chair.

So long as America finds new sub-humans to hate, my three-yearly chore will pose only technical challenges. This fall, it might be homosexuals... or career girls who hold down jobs that ought to go to ex-servicemen... or these new negro-sounding white folk singers.

Juvenile delinquents, though, are off the board. That franchise has been taken for 1954. My red jack has been trumped.

⚹   ⚹   ⚹   ⚹

"They're out to get me, Dr. Carmody," said the fleshy, balding young man who couldn't lie still on the couch. "They want me off newsstands. They want me up before the committee. They want me out of the business."

Sheldon Loesser was a problematic paranoid. It was hard to advise the patient to ignore his imaginary demons... since some of them were real.

He owned High Integrity Comics, publisher of *Morgue of Horror*, *Weird Planet Stories*, *GI Guts,* and other titles. He was also a prolific writer of crime and horror yarns for his own books. Several of my rituals, including the Red Knife business, had been fodder for the "Ghastly—But True!" feature he wrote in HIC's top-seller *Annals of Crime.*

Loesser came to analysis after a reader's parent—upset by "Live Bait," a *Crack of Doom* story about a cruel angler who gets impaled on a giant hook and dangled in a shark tank—wrote to say the writer should have his head examined. The writer duly made an appointment, intending to write it up as an amusing one-page article. The Post Office requires that comics carry a certain amount of text between illustrated stories. In that session, we discovered Loesser was one of life's couch junkies. He relished sorting childhood memories and everyday frustrations to identify the source of every sick idea which cropped up in his eight-page bloodbaths. Chronic insomnia hindered attempts at dream analysis, but his unconscious was poured out in his stories.

At nineteen, he inherited HIC from his father. Mendel Loesser, a funny book pioneer, died unexpectedly, just as the masked hero and amusing animal titles which had made HIC's name were flagging in an oversaturated marketplace. Overnight, the son leaped from office assistant to publisher and sole support of his mother and several sisters. Noticing a sales uptick in crime and horror comics, Loesser concentrated on them. At first through financial necessity, he wrote most of the books himself. He stayed in the office after hours, on liver-abusing quantities of black coffee and pep pills, typing script after script. Younger, hipper, odder, cheaper artists came through the door and HIC became profitable again. Other companies began copying the HIC formula, the ultimate sign of success in comics.

Loesser discovered Jackson Greene, a talented penciller with a bent for the macabre. HIC's busiest artist, Greene signed himself "Gruesome." The most memorable—which is to say, horrible—HIC stories were Loesser-Greene collaborations. They brought out something in each other—more like Leopold and Loeb than Gilbert and Sullivan. I once decorated a room with Mary Kelly's insides, and even I'm disgusted by some things Loesser and Greene have put on paper. It is not the analyst's place to moralise, though.

Despite the increased sales, Loesser was troubled by the thought that Mendel—whose unfulfilled ambition was an illustrated Torah—would have despised the lurid trash which kept the coffers filled. He see-sawed between pride in the work and self-loathing.

Two years into analysis, the patient was reconciled to oedipal feelings about the absent patriarch and the smothering mother. That little cocktail fed many stories about murdered parents clawing out of their graves to avenge themselves on worthless grown-up children. His lingering neuroses worked for him. So long as he was troubled, he had fresh horror ideas—which meant not falling back on plagiarising old radio shows or pulp magazine tales and hoping no one noticed.

No sooner had Loesser gained some sort of equilibrium than the spotlight of the censorious fell on comics and he cracked up again. Now, he was beset by educationalists, church organisations, picketers, and politicians. With his industry under attack, the patient needed two and sometimes three sessions a week.

"It's what the comics are about," he said. "Paying for your sins. The guy who snuffs his father to take over the dry-cleaning business gets flattened in his own press. The dame who swindles the clown gets her guts pulled out like an everlasting string of handkerchiefs. Now, it's the comics' turn to pay… and that guy is the zombie father and the killer clown…"

"That guy," my patient's new nemesis, was Dr. Reuben Hofstedtler, a member of my profession. In magazine articles, a *Reader's Digest* choice best-seller (*The Pied Pipers of Perversion*) and appearances on radio and television shows, Dr. Hofstedtler branded comic books as the root cause of juvenile delinquency. I'd not run into him on the cocktail party circuit, but those who had said he was a man of mystery, perhaps even a fraud. For a start, he was a caricature shrink: Viennese accent, gray beard, thick eyeglasses. He had supposedly given up a lucrative Park Avenue practice to devote himself to his anti-comics campaign, though he still worked downtown in the free clinic for crazy, mixed-up kids where he had formulated his theory. He had noticed that the worst junior hoodlums were readers of mind-rotting stuff like *Annals of Crime* and *Morgue of Horror*, which he described as "play-books for delinquency."

Hofstedtler struck me as a Jekyll-and-Hyde character—sincere in his initial concerns about the not-so-funny funnies, then hopped up on the attention his crusade brought him. He was doing good, altruistic work with young people most of my colleagues wouldn't go near, but turning into a professional pundit brought him a whiff of celebrity. Now, he was hooked on fame. In his own way, he was as well-known as a sports star at the top of their game or an uncaught mystery murderer. Reuben Hofstedtler was the Comic Book Killer.

His methodology was less than scrupulous. A few thin anecdotes cropped up over and over in his articles and broadcasts. They were repeated by everyone else who took up his cause and organised a comics-burning party. A copy of *Weird Planet Stories* was found in the home of a teenager who drowned after driving a stolen Mustang off the Brooklyn Bridge. Three issues earlier, *Weird Planet* ran a story about a Martian crashing a spaceship into an asteroid. Very incriminating… except there was no proof the thief saw the earlier issue or even that the comic in his home was his. He had three younger brothers. And he died drag-racing with other kids who'd stolen cars without prompting from the funnies. Loesser, who had an in with the police sources who kept *Annals of Crime* going, ferreted out the truth of this and other commonly-retold anecdotes. Newspapers which publicised Hofstedtler's "findings" had no interest in covering an evil comic book publisher's refutations.

Reuben Hofstedtler was proof that if you drop enough Freud-and-Jung into your ravings, you can get people to believe anything. Just ask Abner Polk.

"I'll show that shrink, Carmody. I'll see him flayed alive before that committee. Eyes boiled like eggs. Teeth pulled with pliers."

Criticism of comic books had not diminished since Loesser started running stories every other issue in which characters with names like "Robbin Horsetrader" or "Carbon Hosefeathers" suffered horrible yet ironic fates. "Who Heeds the Head-Shrinker?," featured on the cover of the latest *Morgue of Horror*, was the tale of "Dr Huffalingumpus." Having blamed the ills of modern society on the pernicious influence of sinister South American shamans, Dr. H. wakes up on his couch in the last panel with his head literally shrunk. "Mmmm… mmmm…. mmmph," he fumes, trying to squeak a scream through sewn-together lips. The Morgue Meister cackles "guess the Doc really was 'small-minded,' eh, kidettes… heh heh heh!"

I efficiently compartmentalise my life—the secret of psychological health. I am a martini-swilling bachelor man-about-Manhattan, a calculating career criminal, a justice-minded public servant, a registered Democrat for Stevenson, a murderous Hecate worshipper and a dedicated mental health professional—all at the same time. I may write a book, *The Compartmentalized Man*. It would be a best-seller.

Most people let their separate selves bleed into each other, disastrously. Loesser was a champion of constitutionally-guaranteed freedom of speech and a scholar of the literary tradition of Poe, Hawthorne and Henry James… but also an infantile whiner, who responded to any criticism by flinging bloody dung. When commentators said his horror comics were horrible, he loudly denied the charge but wrote more stories like "How to Kill Friends and Mutilate People."

I suggested that venting wrath against Dr. Hofstedtler in four colors was counter-productive. "Who Heeds the Head-Shrinker?" wouldn't win support for Loesser's anti-censorship position, soothe his ulcers, keep him off bennies, or increase sales. Pestered by Hofstedtler's followers, newsstands were returning unsold bales of HIC titles without ever displaying them. Loesser had made personal an argument which could more usefully be conducted dispassionately—which only helped Hofstedtler. At first, for fear of libel or treading on the toes of major publishers who might own a tiny comic book line, Hofstedtler fudged details of the specific comics which drove his patients to crime. Then, he relied on a few out-of-context panels to illustrate articles, or descriptions of particularly appalling incidents which misrepresented grotesque comedy as straightforward sadism.

To keep up the heat, Hofstedtler needed a villain. A Hitler or an Ethel Rosenberg or a Red Knife. A sinister, dangerous mastermind who did intentional harm. Sheldon Loesser fulfilled that role. He was the sweating, wild-eyed face of horror comics. As an in-joke "Gruesome" Greene made the Morgue Meister look like his publisher. This backfired when Loesser became more unkempt. Photographs of him all seemed like mug shots. He perpetually sported that rumpled hair and shifty look of the just-arrested and about-to-be-arraigned.

The last panel of "Who Heeds the Head-Shrinker?" showed Loesser as the Morgue Meister chortling over the fate of Hofstedtler as Huffalingumpus. Another Carmody, tucked away in his compartment, reacted to "Gruesome" Greene's delicately rendered tiny, shrivelled head—with its life-sized panicking eyes, stitched lips and inevitable bone-threaded topknot—by giving vent to a hearty, Hecate-pleasing heh heh heh…

Get the *point*, kidettes?

The session ended at 10:45, signalled by a buzzer loud enough—if needs be, and with some patients they certainly did—to rouse me from a doze. I wrapped things up and ushered Loesser out. A couple of familiar faces loitered in my waiting room. Special Agents Finlay and Dwight.

Kendall Finlay was big, untidier than Hoover liked his G-Men to be, and had a mild, placid look. He was the keener mind, the dangerous man on the team. Healthy and balanced, calm and sceptical. A patient dog-owner, a crossword solver, and a jazz aficionado. I had to be careful with Finlay. Loose threads in the Polk case troubled him. We regularly spitballed possible avenues of further investigation. No results yet, of course. With luck, I could keep steering him away from the unbelievable truth. Marion Dwight was small, dapper, ferret-faced. Cruder, limited, crass. His Mommy stuck him with a girls' name—no matter that it was also John Wayne's—and gave him regular enemas until he was fifteen. Now, he hated women so much he could easily be nudged along shady paths to firm but erroneous conclusions. He'd shot two men and one woman in the line of duty, and been commended for his killings. Finlay confided that he felt any agent who took a life—which he'd never done—should be obliged to undergo analysis, a notion which tickled my interest. I can see advantages in asking the questions and filling in the forms.

Seeing regulation federal agent suits and hats, Loesser started sweating like a junky two days past his last fix. He was expecting a subpoena to appear before the Senate Sub-Committee on Juvenile Crime.

Finlay was considering my Hecate Chiaramonti. The statue, a Roman copy of a Hellenistic original, represents the goddess as three-bodied, like Siamese triplets joined at their backs. Originally, she held pairs of torches, keys, and daggers, but three of the arms were broken off—only a single dagger and the keys remained. Finlay examined the trimorphe statue as if it were evidence, which in certain circumstances it might be. His jacket hung open, showing his shoulder holster.

Dwight was looking sideways at Charmaine, my secretary, hoping there was political significance in her red sweater... imagining her stretched out in a shredded slip on a *Crack of Doom* cover, subjected to the Dread Druid's interrogation techniques.

Loesser got out of the office, sharp-ish... omitting to leave a check with Charmaine, for which we'd bill him interest next time. At least we'd have a new topic for discussion: his fear of the authorities.

Not an irrational fear, though. What kind of a fool *doesn't* fear authorities?

"Jack, sorry to barge in, but we've got another one..." said Finlay.

"A kook case, just the way you like 'em," said Dwight.

I'd expected this. I take all the newspapers. I know the crime sections.

"Come into my parlour, agents," I said. "Charmaine, fend off my eleven o'clock dipso, shift my noonday pansy to next week, and refer this afternoon's shoplifter to Dr. Lark..."

✗   ✗   ✗   ✗

"Your gang war isn't a gang war," I said. "It's a person."

Finlay and Dwight weren't floored by the announcement. They wouldn't have come a-calling if they hadn't worked it out.

We were in my consulting room. Charmaine fended off all comers.

In 1888, Scotland Yard didn't immediately connect the individual Ripper murders. So many women died violently in the rookeries of the East End that my crushed flowers were lost in the crowd. Some offerings escaped the history books because the police—not privy to the ritual—didn't recognise all my tell-tales. One of the "canonical" victims was someone else's kill, the nose-rotted Whitechapel version of Abner Polk settling a score with the drab who gave him the pox.

The same thing was happening now.

Five juvenile delinquents stabbed—four fatally—in the Lower East Side didn't look like one man's work. They were padding the butcher's bill from a long-standing territorial war. The Counts, the Blades, the Shillelagh Boys, and the Hoppers all had men down. Tit-for-tat assaults, rumbles and face-offs spread across the city. Father Molloy, a priest who worked as a missionary among the hoodlums, got the leaders together for a "peace conference." Someone shot him in the face for his pains, so the battles flared again. The toll was in the low twenties so far this year. The wounded overwhelmed local hospitals. An inordinate number of clumsy young men reported accidents with non-serrated bread-knives or cylindrical door-jambs. Little of this bloodshed was of interest. However, someone was out there, shy at present, but growing confident...

"I'm simplifying for effect," I told the agents. "Of course there's a gang war *now*. The police will have to crack heads and fill cells. But that's literally not a federal case. Nevertheless, you're here..."

Finlay and Dwight looked at each other.

"We have a new friend," I announced. "Did he start the wave, or is he surfing it? It doesn't matter. He hides inside the war, like some hide inside fog, taking a boy here and there. Careful to pick off kids from different gangs, so survivors won't talk to each other and sense the beast among them. He wears their colors... or at least can pass in their streets and alleys and vacant lots. My first guess would have been Father Molloy, but he's obviously off the suspect list. We can't rule out a cop or someone else who'd get a pass... a social worker, a delivery boy, even a prostitute. The precision gives him or her away, and serves as a signature. He's in two minds about anonymity. It's necessary if the work is to continue, but every artist wants to read the reviews. He uses his prey's weapon of choice, a switchblade knife... and he's good with it. One insertion, high up in the back, four or five vertebrae down, severing the spinal cord, then a good solid shove. The heads loll forward, like broken dolls. The light goes out in their eyes. Does he look at that, hold up the head by the hair, and try to catch the moment of dying?"

Heh heh heh...

Dwight whistled, impressed.

"You could have called, Jack," said Finlay, almost disappointed in me. "If you were so far ahead. How long have you known?"

I'd shown off. A mistake. But in character for John Carmody, arrogant analyst.

"Not long," I admitted. "The boy who lived, Tino Muñoz, sealed it. Before him, it could have been a fad among a criminal community. Like it was baseball bats to the back of the skull one year... shooting through the femoral artery in that Canadian border tussle... or the Harlem trick with the mailbag and the noose looped around the neck and the feet so the victim wakes up and breaks his own neck."

"Muñoz threw us off," admitted Finlay. "Made the cops think it was what you said, a craze... and not everybody was as good at it as the first guys."

"No, the boy who lived was lucky. The variable was the victim, not the assailant. He gave no useful description but he co-operated with the police, tried to be helpful..."

"I guess being stuck in a bed for the rest of your life loosens even toughies' tongues," said Dwight. "They call him the Talking Head."

Heh heh heh...

"That's a misinterpretation," I said. "If he'd been attacked by someone from a rival gang, Muñoz would have talked to his friends, not the police. Even—no, *especially*—if he knew who it was. These people don't trust cops to avenge them. That Muñoz co-operated suggests this is nothing to do with the social clubs. Street corner society is like the Balkans in 1914. We may not be able to keep track of the alliances, feuds, and brushfire wars, but the players do. Except they don't know what's stalking them. They're children, playing gangsters. This is outside their experience. That makes them easy meat for a predator."

"Think we should let it play out?" said Dwight. "Let him ice a bunch more punks until they get lucky and jump him?"

"Of course not. What our friend—let us call him the Switch-blade Stabber—does is unconscionable. That he chooses to do it to people the mass of our society don't care about is no excuse."

"Like Polk and his commies?" prompted Finlay.

"This is our business," I said. "Extremes of human behaviour. Antisocial extremes. The Stabber thinks of himself as a lone wolf, a hunter thinning out the herd. He may or may not have an inciting incident—a reason to hate juvenile delinquent gangs. There are plenty around. A sister raped, a brother hooked on dope, a family business wrecked by a protection racket. Or he might be one of the curious ones, born crooked or shaped in early childhood to lack something or have a taste for the unspeakable. He may have looked at a map and decided where he could work best."

How did I imagine that? Well, take a wild guess…

"Given the publicity around the Red Knife case, he may be thinking of us. We caught Abner Polk. We were written up in the press, talked about on the radio. There was even a comic book. These stabbings may be a challenge. An opening gambit."

"I miss the way it was in the thirties," said Dwight. "Big-headed morons like Dillinger and Floyd posed with tommy guns for news-paper shutterbugs. You didn't have to work out who they were."

"Director Hoover ranked his public enemies like the record charts," said Finlay. "He called them out. Machine Gun Kelly, Clyde Barrow…"

"The women were the worst," spat Dwight. "Bloody Bonnie, Ma Barker…"

"It was a War on Crime, like the War on the Nazis," said Fin-lay—he had scars from Normandy Beach and a couple of med-als. "Out in the open, guns blazing, bombs flying. This horror, the chess-with-corpses stuff, it's like it is with the reds… a Cold War, fought when no one is looking. Not over things you can understand like land or revenge or money, but about ideas. Stupid ideas."

"Yes, Kendall," I said. "It's all ideas. Which is why you need an idea doctor."

Finlay cracked a smile.

I moved to New York from Chicago in 1949. Cities suit me, obviously. Look at a map of a city and you see my mind. Neighborhoods. Compartments. Grids. Patterns. The rituals of daily life. The rituals of eternal life. Reliable public transport. A high murder rate. I could live here forever.

West 74th St is one Carmody compartment. The Lower East Side is another—though it wasn't somewhere I'd killed. The Red Knife struck all over the city, at a type rather than in a location. Correlations matter, not mere proximity. I could make a string of offerings in one room, so long as the placements were proper. I foresee a future—1984 or 2002, say—when jet-travel is commonplace and I can overlay my grand red design on the map of a country or a continent. Even the globe. Eventually, maybe, in a future of space rangers and rocketmen… across the constellations.

After our discussion, Finlay and Dwight went back to their office. I said I'd work up a dossier on the Switchblade Stabber. They left me with photstats of police reports on the attacks so far, and copies of the criminal records of the victims. Depositions made to the Senate Sub-Committee on Juvenile Crime, including the testimony of battle-scarred Father Molloy, helped fill in the picture. I considered the make-up of New York street gangs in anthropological detail. After spending time with documents, I had an itch to see the hunting ground for myself. I had my calls transferred to the answering service and gave Charmaine the rest of the day off. After pausing for a tiny ritual—nodding three times to Hecate—I shut up my office and went downtown by cab, bus, and on foot.

I wore a Chicago winter coat, fetched from the depths of the closet. I don't stoop to disguises. A good, old coat and a nondescript hat are all I need. You don't fit in, but don't stand out either. Ask me the time or pan-handle me for a dime… and five minutes later you'll do it again without remembering you already hit me up. I have one of those faces. And a gift from the goddess—an inner fog-generator that, as the radio program says, "clouds men's minds."

All slums smell alike. Folks who can't or don't wash enough, rotten fish or vegetables, the stink of opened bowels or veins. People on these streets have the same look as people in Whitechapel in 1888—mostly busy, hustling to make rent or the next meal, but with the odd still, watchful, superior type. Panderers and footpads, once… now, pimps and hoods. And policemen—always policemen. Gangsters and cops have the same stare. This is their territory and they guard it, prepared to repel boarders. Waves of immigrants mean different languages on the streets, many shades of skin color, squabbles and prejudices always on the point of turning nasty… but also intermarriage, assimilation, that famous melting pot.

The last war here was between Vampires and Dragons.

Now, there were more gangs, clubs, and splinter groups than a sociologist could keep track of. Our new friend, though—he was well-informed. The Counts, the Blades, the Shillelagh Boys, and the Hoppers were Polish, Puerto Rican, Irish, and Negro. They fought over a few city blocks. Grown-up crime was monopolised by Jews and Italians… but the established, complacent mobs were starting to lose ground to upstart crews with sharper knives and newer ideas.

In Whitechapel, I was the cause of an unprecedented truce. Mobs who'd been killing each other for over a hundred years found common cause with the hated peelers… and set out to find and stop me. You know how that worked out. By 1891, when I did it all over again—using the underground railway to extend my design across the whole city—the gangs were back to cutting each other's throats and coshing fools who nipped into the wrong pub. For all the fuss made about the Ripper, almost no one—I except Guy Hollis's deluded father—even noticed the repeat performance three years later.

I did a tour of the current crimes. Five sites. Five stabbings.

On the map, an inelegant grouping—these were attacks of opportunity, not offerings at altars. On the ground—narrow alleys, gaps between tenement houses, a junk lot, a trash area behind a bar.

It was like coming home. Part of me is drawn to these anonymous places. By day, they were busy… but the stabbings were after dark. There must have been witnesses. There always are in crowded quarters like this. But this fellow was quick, didn't need to take his time. Only one of his attacks was botched. I figured people saw him strike, well away from working street-lamps, but didn't realise what they'd witnessed.

The gangs were all over. Knots of youths, lounging on street corners, smoking cigarettes, combing their hair, cat-calling girls, slapping each other, playing cards or knife-games. Different colors for different factions. The Counts had black leather jackets and motorcycle boots, though few owned bikes or cars—if they needed wheels, they stole them. The Blades wore colorful silk jackets and drape pants with thin-brimmed hats and parakeet ties. They were growing prosperous—if you wanted dope, you bought it from them. The Hoppers, poorer and less numerous, made do with blue jeans, white t-shirts, and army surplus coats. The Boys wore the green, if unobtrusively, and clustered around businesses—bars, machine shops, stores, a church hall—run by older brothers or parents. They put up a show of force but were eager to move off the street and into warm offices, to count rather than collect the money, to go into politics and the big-time rackets. Like the Jews and the Italians.

A lot of kids were reading comic books published by Sheldon Loesser and his competitors. An observation which might have interested Dr. Hofstedtler, though it went against the prevailing tide of his research, was that crime and horror comics were popular but as many toughs read funny animal or costumed adventurer books. The pundit found it harder to work up rage against those, though a chapter of *The Pied Pipers of Perversion* explored the notion that the adult-hero-and-young-sidekick relationship typified by Batman and Robin peddled pederasty to the masses. Loitering all day is a spur to reading of all kinds. I saw Blades comparing their haircuts to Tony Curtis's in movie fan magazines, boys of all ethnicities devouring the latest Mickey Spillane, and a Hopper half-way through a library copy of Booth Tarkington's *The Ambersons*.

The files on the victims listed items found on their persons at the time of death. I wondered if the bland category "reading matter" meant comic books. It could as easily refer to newspapers, motorcycle magazines, or Pulitzer prize-winning novels of yesteryear.

Was the Switchblade Stabber an addict of *Annals of Crime*? He was certainly pitching for a "Ghastly—But True" feature.

Evening came on. Market carts pushed off and sweatshops let out. More people on the streets. An easier crowd to hide in.

Cooking smells seeped from the tenements. Radios and gramophones gave the factions their own musical accompaniment—sentimental songs for nose-slitting young warriors.

I walked casually, talked to no one, bought nothing, didn't linger.

My bargain with Hecate isn't just for a long life and clean complexion. I have other senses, acquired or developed in the dark. It's how I found Abner Polk.

I cast about for the Switchblade Stabber.

Was he near?

He must be tall. Strong. Practiced and precise, despite the slip with the Talking Head. In the prime of life. Not previously known to the police, unless for something trivial... some start with animals or self-harm, or indecent exposure, even arson or trophy-theft. Killers of women filch brassieres or stays from clotheslines... what might a killer of teenage hoodlums steal? Gang colors, combs, emblems, weapons? Older than his victims, but with status among them. A perceived neutral. Molloy fit my profile perfectly, but two of the Stabber's victims had been put down after his shooting—which he'd survived, being a tough old mick. A beat cop? A patrolman might get kids off the main street with a shake-down or an arrest or an interrogation, then strike.

Tino Muñoz was no help—he was hazy about the circumstances, and described "an old guy with a nice voice." To a seventeen-year-old, an "old guy" could be in his twenties or thirties. And what was a "nice voice?" I didn't think to send Finlay and Dwight after George Sanders.

The rumour-mill suggested the Ripper was a policeman, a mad surgeon, a butcher, or a midwife... the public, and Queen Victoria, wanted him to be a foreigner. A Chinese hatchet man, a demented Lascar, a Hottentot cannibal with filed teeth. An American, even...

Free-form noise and scented smoke leaked out of a basement club on Delancey Street. A new cultural enclave. Places like this were more common uptown, or in the Village. Another of my compartments—John Carmody, bohemian. I was comfortable around sculptors with beards and berets, lady poets with matador pants and sunglasses after dark, prose writers who didn't use punctuation or apostrophes, and visionaries who scratched celluloid strips and projected the results like movies. A few might aspire to be my patients. Not that they wanted to be cured. Under the shadow of the H-bomb, they clung to craziness like an umbrella. It made them creative.

I slipped into the joint just as a guy in a Hawaiian shirt finished a monologue accompanied by two cats on bongos and an alto sax. He shut up but the music loped on, asymmetric and atonal and, like, crazy, man...

There was a press of people. I was pushed against a wall papered with pages from HIC comics, lumpy with paste. The Morgue Meister, the Dread Druid, Commander Planet and the others were there, over and over, images from the reverse of the pages leaking through. Guillotined magicians' assistants... bug-eyed monsters from Planet Weird... that pressed-flat coat-presser... that shrunken head shrink... *GI Guts* spilled over atolls and beaches and numbered hills... neck-snapped Harlem squealers in mail-bags... vampires and dragons versus Vampires and Dragons... public enemies cut down by G-men with tommy guns... one-page riffs to appease the post office... the red red Red Knife, cutting commie throats... black men in oversized coats hanging from lamp-posts surrounded by chanting hooded fiends... ads for physical education, x-ray specs, American seeds, and hypnotists who could cure a stammer or introduce you to girls. All the images bled into each other. The compartment walls were breaking down.

Too many people here were smoking stuff that wasn't strictly tobacco.

I was fixating on the comic book panels.

Click. The Carmody in charge, the king of the compartments, took over.

This wasn't a Stabber haunt. Not yet. These non-conformists were a group, not a gang.

I withdrew, but the comic book collage stuck in the mind. It was like one of my designs on a map.

A labyrinth, like the streets round here.

As if by free association, I went from the basement club to a waste-ground. Blades and their girls danced to mambo music. They ignored me. This was a mating ritual, not a sacrifice.

Then, I found a cinder-block building on Ludlow Street. New and ugly, like a military outpost in just-conquered territory. A free clinic. They had them in Whitechapel too. I recognised the address.

Tino Muñoz had been brought here, though there was nothing to do for him but call an ambulance. The place was busy with cuts and bruises.

A thirteen-year old, green ribbon pinned to his jacket, bawled like an infant as a nurse washed a long cut on his arm, which had gone through his sleeve to the meat. He wasn't hurt seriously enough to let inside. The sister wore whites and had a starched hat perched in her bottle blonde perm. She must have been forty, but still in the game. Not a nun.

"You hurt, mister?" she asked me.

She was the first person in the neighborhood to notice me watching. I almost revised my thinking. A nurse would have to be strong, might be trusted enough by gang kidettes, could get behind and above with a switchblade.

If she wore a man's suit and hat, could a nurse be "an old guy with a nice voice?"

It was unlikely to be that easy.

I shrugged and said nothing. The woman got back to her patient.

"We'll get 'em back, Sean," said an older youth, also green-ribboned. "The hunkies it was. We'll get 'em back."

The nurse cuffed Sean's friend and told him not to be any more of a fool than God made him.

"Here," she said, after the job was done, producing a lollipop from a pocket, "get this in your gob to shut you up. And go home, you little idjits."

She let the bandaged wonder be hauled off and went back inside.

I wondered what her name was and sidled up to a shingle that listed the staff.

She was either Miss Maire O'Connell, APN, or Mrs. Bridgit Cohen, RN.

… but those names faded. Another leapt out.

Psychiatric Case Worker—Dr Reuben Hofstedtler, APsaA, APA, NYPSI, M.D., et cetera.

I whistled.

⚔ ⚔ ⚔ ⚔

The next morning, Joseph Mapp—a Hopper—was listed as the Stabber's sixth.

Finlay brought the news to my office. He and Dwight went over the reports every day, winnowing out the Stabber's doings from general routine carnage.

Mapp was found dead two streets from the clinic, face down in a copy of *Crack of Doom*. From mug-shots, I recognised the boy I'd seen engrossed in *The Ambersons*. I wasn't sure I believed his eclectic tastes in "reading matter." The cops had hauled in Sean Hogan (of the slit sleeve) and his brother Michael and were grilling them lightly. I could have told the police the Irish boys' beef was with "hunkies" not Mapp's colored gang, but wasn't keen on admitting I'd been there. If you're seen at the sites of murders, people get ideas...

... no, it would *not* be hilarious to get away with 138 murders over sixty-five years, then get pinched for crimes I *didn't* commit. It was the sort of nasty turn Sheldon Loesser used too often. In the horribly moral world of the comics, merciless cosmic justice undid the wrongdoer. Why didn't Dr Hofstedtler notice the square crime-does-not-pay messages? In the real universe, Hecate rewards her devotees.

Mapp was killed after midnight, when I was back in my apartment. The murder could not be said to have been committed "under my nose." But had I been noticed? We watch, we predators. We are perceptive. If our friend had seen me but I'd not seen him, he was more dangerous than I'd assumed. The nurse? Someone in the beat club? An invisible old Jewish or Italian guy?

Surely, there couldn't be another moon-worshipper in the city? From the evidence, the ritual was all wrong. But evidence could be partial, or not looked at from the right, skewed angle. I needed to do more research. Behind respectable shelves of psychiatry journals and text-books, I keep arcana like Prinn's *Mysteries of the Worm* and Balfour's *Cults of Ghouls*. The occult is another of my compartments.

Finlay showed me stark crime scene photos. That's how I noticed the *Crack of Doom* issue. It had fallen flat, so the cover was splayed out—a leprous drooling creature, splattered with Joseph Mapp's real blood. If Reuben Hofstedtler needed a shock image for the jacket of a sequel to *The Pied Pipers of Perversion*, this was a shoo-in. That made me wonder whether that wasn't the whole point of the stabbings. Someone might be making Hofstedtler's case for him, more forcefully than a syndicated radio broadcast.

Should I share my tentative idea with Finlay? It was a long-shot.

I couldn't see the elderly, bespectacled Dr. Hofstedtler striking down teenage toughs, no matter how many anatomy charts he studied. Still, he cropped up all over this story. His crusade was in the news while the Senate Sub-Committee was in session. He might have disciples. Also, and this gave me shivers, the doctor was younger than me. I, of all people, shouldn't underestimate the physical capacity of an educated man.

I put Mapp's crime scene photo on my desk and lined up similar shots from the other stabbings.

"What do you see?" Finlay asked.

"Nothing yet," I said.

But there they were. *Annals of Crime. Morgue of Horror. Crack of Doom. Dick Squad.* Stuck in jacket or jeans pockets, crumpled up and lying around, sometimes just a torn page. The police hadn't made the connection. Comic books were everywhere, after all. So were gum wrappers and newspapers and used bus tickets and handbills for local businesses. I could probably find those at all the death scenes, too.

Hofstedtler's big theory was that comics turn kids into killers… but the upshot of the Stabber's work seemed to mark kids who read comics as murder victims. Acts like these have personal meaning—blessed be the Goddess of the Crossways—to the perpetrator. This was something to do with the funny books.

Finlay looked at the same photographs. He kept going back to Mapp.

"This isn't how he fell," said the Special Agent, at last. "He's been shifted… you can see where the scuff-marks are. His head has been placed on the magazine. Like a pillow."

"It's not a magazine," I prompted.

"Oh yes, I see. A comic book. Kids' stuff. Looking at them dead and going over their rap sheets, you forget how young they were. Mapp was fifteen. This monkey has got to be stopped, John."

I agreed with Special Agent Finlay.

The Mid-Town offices of High Integrity Comics were above Loesser & Son's print works. Mendel Loesser, originally a printer, lost clients in the 1930s when *bund* lobbyists persuaded some companies not to use "Jewish firms" to run off cracker packets and candy wrappers. He turned publisher to keep his presses rolling. Comic books were even cheaper to throw together than pulp magazines. The sickly kids who wrote and drew them knew less than wordsmiths about contracts, rights, and payments.

Thanks to the circumstances of HIC's origins, their first heroes—the mysterious Moon Mask, the mesmeric Madame Violet, and two-fisted Doc Gargantua—fought Nazis well before America entered the War. The adventurers rose to popularity on a wave of patriotic bloodthirstiness. Mostly retired now, the numbering of their books continued. The fee for registering a new title doesn't have to be paid if an old comic just changes its name and direction. *Morgue of Horror* begun as *Moon Mask Mysteries* in 1938 and had been *Moon Mask Funnies*, *Moonlight Romance*, and *Moon of Horror* along the way. *Madame Violet* was now *Annals of Crime*. The former cover star still hosted a back-up feature about murderesses, "Deadly Dames and Dastardly Dolls."

This was my first visit to my patient's workplace. It was like stepping from one compartment to another.

I introduced myself to Loesser's secretary, an old stick who didn't have Charmaine's curves. Beyond a wood-and-frosted-glass partition, her boss cackled like the Morgue Meister. The secretary let me pass without a grilling. I found Loesser and a smartly-dressed young man poring over artwork in which an old gent with thick glasses was getting throttled by his own beard, which had turned into a writhing nest of snakes. Sheldon Loesser, a quivering wreck on my couch, was a confident dictator in his own realm.

"Hi, Dr. C.," said Loesser, far more relaxed than when I'd last seen him. "Have you met Jackson Greene? The Norman Rockwell of slaughtered families. The Vargas of decapitated showgirls."

So this was the legendary "Gruesome." You'd never think to see him that he was capable of his art. Some might say that of me.

Greene snapped off a military salute and said "pleased to meet you, sir."

Loesser pencilled notes in margins. He kept having ideas. He threw his thoughts my way as well as at his artist.

"How about a comic about analysis?" he said. "Instead of the Morgue Meister or the Dread Druid, we could have a head-shrinker host. Dr. Alan List? *Tales From the Couch*. You up for endorsing that, Dr. C.? Could you open your files? We like 'authenticated cases' at HIC."

"There'd be ethical concerns," I said.

He wasn't disappointed. And skipped on to the next thought. "Maybe a book about cavaliers and duellists?"

I was here to see if I could firm up the connection between comic books and the Switchblade Stabber rather than as part of the analytic process. However, a picture above Loesser's desk told me something that ought to have been a breakthrough. First, I wondered why my patient had a photograph of his arch-enemy on display... then I saw that the thick-spectacled, bearded, disapproving old fellow in the black-bordered frame was not Dr. Reuben Hofstedtler but the firm's founder, the Loesser of Loesser & Son. Mendel greatly resembled Hofstedtler. So, this was why Loesser took the anti-comics campaign so personally and responded with such vicious stories. It was transference, an identification of the troublesome foe with the distant father, who was dead and would therefore never give his son the approval he craved.

Hofstedtler could have been Mendel Loesser's brother.

No one knew Hofstedtler's family background—or even if Hofstedtler was his real name. Could this whole comic book kerfuffle be an oedipal story writ large? Did that extend to the Stabber?

Greene and Loesser went through a whole issue of *Morgue*— four stories, all drawn by Greene, all written by Loesser.

"Gorgon Beard" was the lead-off, and Greene had already provided cover art. There was a tale about an escaped homicidal maniac serving cyanide to barroom bores... "What's Your Poison?" One of a series about a shambling creature composed of a downed German bomber crew and a mystic fungus, "The Mass Strikes." And a standard anecdote about an unheeding anthropologist who falls foul of an ancient moon cult... "What the Hecate!"

Naturally, the last story piqued my interest. I didn't let it show.

"Know where I got the idea from, Doc?" Loesser asked.

I shrugged, coolly.

"You," he said.

I had a scalpel in my pocket—I always did—its blade encased in a cork.

"In your reception room, you have that hunk of statue. It's a Hecate. Three women in one. What a nightmare! I looked the old hag up. We're always looking for cults. We've done voodoo too often. And plain old Satanism is just as tired."

"I wanted Hecate on the cover," said Greene. "But Mr. Loesser prefers the chin-gorgon. Do you collect such things, doctor?"

"I know what the statue is, but it has no particular significance," I lied. "A present from a patient. Some say analysis is a modern cult. People come to me the way they once went to priests. As channels to hidden wisdom. To help them change their lives."

I only now noticed a glint in Greene's eye. On the street, you'd take him for a young exec. If he were carrying a portfolio, it would be art for a brand of vermouth or new cool-tasting cigarettes. Not multi-limbed mushroom masses or disturbingly accurate pagan sacrifices. The glint was what made him "Gruesome." Another compartmentalized man. Like poor outmoded Moon Mask, he had a secret identity. Like me, John-better-known-as-Jack.

Greene was slight, compact. Smooth-shaven. In a wig and dress, he could pass for a woman. He was tense—chewing gum as if it were a serious business, making strange knuckle-cracking gestures. He had artists' hands. He could shade a line perfectly, but maybe also punch through brick.

Loesser let it all out… on the couch, in his stories.

Greene just had his art. So far as I knew.

One thing Loesser expressed in the early days of his analysis—before Dr. Hofstedtler manifested as his nightmare nemesis and crowded out all his other concerns—was guilt over the industry-standard wretched deal HIC gave its artists. Thanks to contracts drawn up by Mendel Loesser's lawyers in a more innocent age, anyone working for HIC who wasn't in the Loesser family got royally shafted—poor up-front payment, no royalties, no participation in ownership of characters and stories, not even the return of artwork. Greene, whose style was as unique as his "Gruesome" signature, was HIC's outstanding artist but earned only pennies.

Once, Loesser had been agonised by the possibility that Greene—upon whom his whole line depended—would desert HIC and land a better-paying syndicated newspaper strip. Now, of course, no newspaper would touch anyone tainted with horror comics and Greene was stuck in a fast-shrinking ghetto. If Hofstedtler got his way, Loesser would at least still own a print shop. "Gruesome" would be gone, man, gone...

Though Greene and Loesser seemed to collaborate amicably, their relationship must be complicated. If Greene could afford analysis, it'd be interesting to know what seethed under his crew-cut... besides murdering Reuben Hofstedtler over and over in print, he had a habit of working caricatures of a dismembered or mutilated Sheldon Loesser into stories. The Morgue Meister took his horror lumps every issue.

I wanted—more than ever after seeing Mendel's picture—to know about the feud between Loesser and Hofstedtler. On the couch, my patient told me how he *felt*... now I wanted facts, not feelings. Where did this hostility come from, specifically? How had the enemies first met? *Had* they met? I know Loesser offered to debate with Hofstedtler in the public forum of his choice, but the pundit didn't bite... he wanted to preach, not argue.

Before I could ask anything, a commotion began beyond the partition.

Breaking glass, shouting, the secretary's high, thin scream.

We rushed out of Loesser's den. It was all I could do not to pull my scalpel.

A man lay broken-backed on a desk, on fire. He had leaped or been thrown through a big window. The glass was smashed in-wards. Wind and noise blew in, lifting papers off desks. People out on the street were chanting something.

A man in shirt-sleeves and tie—an art editor, I think—dumped a bucket of sand on the burning figure, smothering the flames. It was an articulated dummy. Comic books were tacked to it, like armour or decoration. They had been lit before the thing was cata-pulted into the HIC offices.

"That bastard," exclaimed Loesser. "He's behind this! Hofst-edtler! It's just a step from burning comics to burning comics writ-ers..."

"...and artists," said Greene, quietly.

Loesser was red-faced, infuriated, raving. Greene smiled grimly, looking at the smoking human piñata. It was like a British Guy Fawkes dummy or a waxwork witch.

What did he see through the eyes of "Gruesome?"

Someone had the presence of mind to telephone the police.

I looked through the broken window. Outside on the sidewalk was an angry parents' group, holding up placards bearing anti-comic book slogans. "HIC = Hellish Infernal Cr**!" "Protect Our Children—Ban Horror and Crime!" "Comics Kill!" They were burning more comics in barbeques brought along for the purpose. Mostly middle-aged women, with a few male long-hairs in the mix and a couple of bruisers who had the whiff of hired muscle. The cops had already shown, but no one owned up to tossing the burning dummy.

"The coward's not here, you note," said Loesser. "Hofstedtler's never at these Klan meets. Does the broadcasts and the articles and lets shills and minions do the street thuggery. It's the *bund* all over again."

I looked at the crowd of shouting faces.

Was the Stabber out there? It would fit his profile.

"This is why the work is important," said Greene.

...or was our new friend this side of the lines?

✗   ✗   ✗   ✗

Finlay and Dwight caught up with me after office hours, in a diner. We took a booth and again went over the state of the Stabber investigation. The papers were spread out on the table. Dwight side-glanced at the waitress, hungry for more than chili. Finlay was focused on the case, but frustrated—lots of developments, but no progress.

"So someone else noticed the comic books?" I said.

"Or wants the connection made," Finlay observed, shrewdly.

The protest at the HIC offices was prompted by press reports linking the death toll on the Lower East Side—all of it, not just the Stabber's take—to comic books. The papers didn't yet know there was such a person as the Switchblade Stabber. But they had crime scene photographs of dead kids with comics.

Finlay blamed cops for letting the pictures get in circulation.

I understood the friction between the FBI and the NYPD. Whitechapel was on the borderline between the jurisdictions of two different police forces who wasted time going over each other's work, squabbling about procedure and missing the obvious. That had worked to my advantage. I now deliberately sought such hinterlands. The police had enough trouble keeping a lid on the gang war and didn't even want to admit there was a calculating murderer in the mix. Unless results showed up soon, Finlay and Dwight would be pulled off the Stabber and assigned to non-phantom cases.

Some helpful citizen had written anonymous letters to the papers claiming that comic books were behind the violence on the streets. Not so long ago, they would have been filed in the wastepaper basket. In this climate, they got printed.

Hofstedtler was all over it. He was quoted, mostly from his book. Loesser, self-appointed representative of "the industry" was allowed to respond. His quotes ran under pictures of him looking like a public enemy and blown-up "Gruesome" panels.

One rag ran a centre-spread alternating the crime scene photographs with climactic images from crime and horror comics. Actual pictures of murdered children were deemed less offensive than drawings of vampires and famous criminals. The paper had found a way to run both, while condemning HIC for pandering to ghoulish tastes.

"This garbage shouldn't be allowed," said Dwight. "For kids."

"Have you got anything on who the Stabber might be?" asked Finlay.

"I've gone over everything and worked up a profile," I said.

The agents looked eager. At this stage in the Red Knife investigation, I had presented them with a detailed description of Abner Polk that listed everything about him but his name. I figured they hoped for another miracle.

"Our man is about sixty, but rugged," I began. "Not physically appealing, under average height... white, protestant, American— probably with German or Swiss ancestors... unmarried, with deeply repressed homosexual tendencies—perhaps with a long-term male best friend, but most likely celibate... reveres his mother, and thinks of her as a saint no other woman could match... in a job with official authority, but frustrated by limitations placed on him by the law... wild rumours circulate about commonplace perversions—transvestism, sado-masochism—but they are exaggerations, people around him picking up on desires he could never act on... vain, obsessed with position—the type who looks through the papers and listens to the radio, poring over every mention of him... jealous of others who achieve prominence in his line of work, and willing to undermine or betray them, especially when it's imputed he lacks the courage they display in the field while he collects honors from behind a desk... paranoid about his position, prone to using blackmail, backroom influence and edge-of-illegal methods to maintain it... petty, vindictive, fanatical about others' appearance... prejudiced against ethnic minorities... a staunch patriot, yet willing to ignore constitutional liberties... a stutterer who overcompensates by speaking rapidly, stressing odd words... a Freemason."

✗   ✗   ✗   ✗

Having set Finlay and Dwight on the trail of J. Edgar Hoover, I finished my steak and again made my way downtown.

One name kept cropping up all over this case—but I'd still not met Dr. Reuben Hofstedtler. Time I got the measure of my professional colleague. He had a hand in the game, somehow. A hand with a red jack showing.

Crusader against horror comics. Radio "personality." Selfless psychiatrist. Mendel Loesser lookalike. Caricature Freudian.

Yet another compartmentalized man.

And maybe a fraud.

Hofstedtler's shingle listed his affiliations. APsaA, APA, NYPSI. However, the directories of the American Psychoanalytic Association, American Psychological Association and New York Psychoanalytic Society—all prominently displayed in my office— didn't list him. I had called the APsaA membership secretary and been told Hofstedtler had a pending application, but his paperwork wasn't yet complete. The little formality of establishing his credentials and qualifications (if any) remained to be tidied up. It's not so hard to furnish the corroborating degrees and records to get a listing. My own directory entry is convincing, though it doesn't cite the actual medical qualifications I obtained in 1883. Same story at the APA and NYPSI. I even wondered about Hofstedtler's

M.D.—supposedly earned in Vienna. Thanks to Anschluss, the War, the deportation and murder of the Jewish population, and partition by the occupying powers, Vienna was one of the best cities in the world to have records lost or destroyed. Yet Hofstedtler was trusted by everyone. He had the accent, after all. And the beard.

He could be reached via his booking agent, but the only place Hofstedtler seemed to hang his hat—and then only on a part-time basis—was the Ludlow Street Clinic. Did he live there? Kept warm in a backroom by a pile of burning comics?

On my previous visit, he was absent. The slot by his shingle for a "the doctor is in" plaque was empty. I didn't really expect him to be there at eleven o'clock in the evening, but I figured I could get into his office and rifle through it for clues about where to find him.

I'm not a detective, obviously. I'm a doctor. And a murderer.

Never forget. Yours ever, Jack the Ripper.

One more stabbing hadn't changed anything. The district was still busy, and the alleys still open for business. There didn't even seem to be more cops about. Indeed, there were notably few uniformed officers within several blocks of the pool parlour where the Blades and the Counts were carving each other up. A semi-official rumble. Someone had taken the trouble to crank up a jukebox. Thumps, slashes, and screams mixed in with the racket of that new novelty hit "We're Gonna Rock Around the Clock Tonight."

The stink of fresh-spilled blood was in the air.

I gripped my scalpel in my pocket.

I didn't *need* to make an offering, but… September chill was setting in. The leaves were turning. Soon, it would be fall.

Circuitously, I approached Ludlow Street. The clinic would be overwhelmed soon, with broken heads and cut faces.

Then, another player popped up unexpectedly.

If not for habitual caution, I'd have tripped over him.

Another stranger on these streets, going my way. Slight, neat, with a portfolio under his arm. Jackson Greene.

Gruesome.

Did he sketch from life?

From across the lot, I watched the artist walk up to the clinic, have a brief talk with the nurse, and be allowed in.

Had he claimed to be injured? Or neurotic and in need of analysis? One glimpse of his portfolio might be enough to earn him a serious head-shrinking.

I waited a few minutes, for the first of the casualties—a Count with his nose mashed flat by a pool-cue, hefted by two of his comrades—to be admitted. Then came a rowdy crowd. I pulled my hat down, held my face as if it were bleeding, and slipped inside with the mob.

The injured from both sides came to the same place, which set off the rumble again. My favorite nurse tried to shout down the bickering, combustible kids. Two went for each other, and she had to wrestle them apart—which she did with practiced ease.

I took advantage of this distraction to slide down a dark corridor, away from the busy emergency room. The psychiatric case worker's office was signposted.

I hadn't been able to see the shingle, so I didn't know whether Hofstedtler was in. But I had a pretty good notion someone else was.

I stood outside his door. A rim of light leaked under it.

Listening, I heard a scuffle of sorts going on. Then quiet.

Standing to one side—the Stabber favored a switchblade for his pleasure but that didn't rule out his carrying a gun for convenience—I kicked the door open, took a quick look to make sure it was safe and stepped in.

It was a small, bare consulting room—shelves with books, framed newspaper articles about the evils of comics, and an open back-door into another dark, glistening alley.

Oh, and a couch. On it lay Jackson "Gruesome" Greene, with a letter-opener in his neck. He was pouring out his troubles, more literally than most patients. He was one of his own final panels, spattered red, eyes fish-wide and dimming.

Like me, he'd come here for an answer—presumably, to the question of "why are you wrecking my livelihood, you demented quack?" And found a different ending.

I revised my opinion of Reuben Hofstedtler. How old and frail was he really?

✗   ✗   ✗   ✗

I left the clinic by Hofstedtler's private door, and walked carefully down the alley. It was narrow, and had several blind kinks. This hidden exit was kept clear, as if well-used. I could see the advantages.

Hofstedtler—if that was who had done for Greene—had no reason to think anyone else was coming after him. Except he'd just committed murder. Murderers, no matter how well-practiced, *always* think someone's coming after them. It may be an externalisation of deeply-suppressed guilt. But everyone on the street looks like a cop. Or an infernal avenger.

I found myself in a cramped courtyard. Three buildings showed windowless backs. It could have been Whitechapel in the last century.

Standing under a fire escape was my quarry. Moonlight glinted off his thick glasses.

"I vas vaiting for you, Doctor Carmody," he said. "Ve haff much to talk off, haff we not?"

I recognised the voice of Reuben Hofstedtler.

He showed me his empty hands. No switchblade.

"I knew you'd understand," he said.

The wig, the glasses, and the beard came off.

"I had to do it, Doc," said Sheldon Loesser.

This was certainly a breakthrough. Torn by hate and love for his cold father, wracked with pride and guilt about his work, he'd become a classic partitioned personality... a self divided and dangerously at war, literally campaigning against his own best interests, artistically murdering himself over and over again. When that didn't resolve anything, he set out to prove his point by linking horror and crime comics with real horror and crime. It was interesting and unusual that his secondary self had attained a degree of success independent of the originating personality, but—of course—Sheldon Loesser was a talented writer.

The compartmentalized man should take care his selves can co-exist. When they rub against one another, like sandpaper or flint, fires start. The compartments collapse. The whole man can be destroyed.

"We'll have to go to the police, Sheldon," I told him. "Doctor-patient privilege doesn't cover... well, murder."

Then, Loesser's face changed again. He was Hofstedtler and Loesser at the same time… and also the Morgue Meister.

"Heh heh heh…"

He actually said "heh heh heh." It scraped the nerves.

"But we *can't* go to the police, John," he said. "Your goddess wouldn't permit it. Did you think no one would ever recognise Hecate? That no one else would read the grimoires, would understand your private ritual? "Ghastly—But True." We researched that feature thoroughly. Sometimes, the truth is too ghastly for *Annals of Crime. Morgue of Horror* should have a "Horrid—But True" feature. We could fit you in there, John. Or should I call you Jack? Nimble Jack, Slippery Jack, Saucy Jack, Cunning Jack, Red Jack… Did you like the way we handled your last ritual? 'Comrades, Quake in Fear of the Red Knife: The Abner Polk Story.' We should have given you a co-writing credit. All the other killers you've been, John… the Butchers, the Beasts, the Stalkers, the Slashers, the Stranglers. The Voo-Doo Man, the Cleveland Torso Slayer. All the other cities, from Milan to Adelaide. And the first offerings, the sacrifices that *took*, the gutted girls that keep your face smooth. You are Jack the Ripper."

I had underestimated my patient. I admit it.

Always, I have had an urge to sign my work. I didn't write letters, but I would have if I'd thought of it. I'd left enough traces for someone with Loesser's peculiar interests to catch up.

"Don't you see, John… we're alike. We both murder for a cause."

"You're nothing like me," I said. "I kill because I must, to keep my part of a bargain. You—well, you kill because…"

He smiled, in anticipation of praise.

"Because you're a nut!"

I might have slapped him. His eyes went wide with shock.

"A nut, Sheldon. A pitiful nut.'

Not as fancy as I usually put it, I admit. But a diagnosis I'd stand by.

Hand in pocket, I flicked the cork off the blade of my scalpel. I stepped towards Loesser. His back was against a wall.

"You're wrong," he insisted. "I see vot you are, vot's inside you. I zhrink your head, I see ze red stuff churning. Ve should be colleagues, Dr. Carmody. I've found out zo much about you. I know everyzing!"

"You think you know me," I whispered, producing the scalpel. "You don't know Jack."

Kim Newman is a prolific, award-winning English writer and editor, who also acts, is a film critic, and a London broadcaster. Of his many novels and stories, one of the most famous is *Anno Dracula*.

GATES OF BAKER STREET

by Mackenzie Clarkes

In, London's streets
The oak doors
Of Baker Street
Stands, a beacon,
To forgotten days
When carriages
From Scotland Yard
Rolled to call
On Mister Holmes
In his lodgings

BUS-TED

by Laird Long

Martelli spat out his toothpick. Grogan swung his feet off the desk as the bus driver walked into the homicide bureau.

"Over here, Adams. Take a seat," Detective Martelli said.

The nervous-looking man in the blue Transit uniform sat down, twisted his hands in his lap. "What's this all about, officers? My dispatcher said you—"

"We've got a guy in the other room name of Todd Benton," Martelli informed Adams. "His estranged wife was murdered at 5:40 tonight. In back of the flower shop she worked at on Sixth Street. Co-worker heard a scream, saw a man running off down the alley. Benton says it wasn't him, he was on the number 24 bus headed home from the office, didn't get off until he hit the 'burbs."

Detective Grogan picked it up, "Benton claims he caught the 24 at the corner of Constitution Avenue and Second Street, at 5:26, one of the first stops on that route. You were at the wheel of that bus at that time, Adams. Your dispatcher told us so. We want to see if you can identify Benton, back up his story."

"Well, uh, I get so many passengers… at rush hour." Adams jumped his shoulders up and down.

"This character has a real memorable face," Grogan told the driver. "And he travels regular every day, he says."

"Well, uh, it was actually my first time on the 24 route, officer, so I don't know any of the regulars. And—and I only went up to Middletown Mall, on Twelfth Street. Then I was relieved by another driver. You see, I was just filling in after completing my own regular route. I didn't go all the way to the end of the line—out into the suburbs."

Martelli grunted. "So maybe you saw this guy get off the bus at Sixth Street when you made your stop at 5:32?"

"They get off at the back door, officer, I can't really see them very well," Adams protested. "The bus is crowded. And it gets dark early now. The bus isn't very well-lit."

"Bring Benton in here!" Martelli barked at the uniformed officer standing by the door.

The two detectives glowered at the bus driver. He stared down at his hands.

The door was opened by the officer, and a man dressed in a dark business suit and open grey trenchcoat was led up to the detectives' desk. He had a large, round, purple birthmark on his otherwise pale right cheek.

"Recognize this man?" Grogan asked Adams.

The driver glanced up at Benton. "Well, uh, I'm not—"

"Sure you remember me!" Todd Benton said eagerly. "I got on your bus at Constitution and Second, rode it all the way out to Oak Street out in Westwood. Just a few stops from your last stop at Heritage Arena."

"Okay, yeah… maybe," Adams said uncertainly. "Your, uh, face does look *kind* of familiar."

Martelli snorted. "Did he see you get off the bus at your home stop, Benton? Did you get off at the front?"

"No, I went out the back door. And I noticed he was busy checking the traffic in the next lane as I left."

"So, how about it, Adams?" Martelli asked. "Did you give a ride to this guy at the time of the murder, or didn't you?"

"Uh…"

"Doesn't matter," Grogan told his exasperated partner. Then surprised the detective and the bus driver even more by adding, "Benton just gave himself away."

"How!?" all three other men chorused.

Detective Grogan said, "Simple. Benton indicated that Adams was the bus driver all the way along Route 24. But Adams told us he'd been relieved by another driver partway along the route, at the Twelfth Street stop. You would've known that, Benton, had you actually ridden that bus all the way out to Oak Street in the suburbs, as you claimed. Instead of getting off earlier to murder your wife."

Benton made a break for the door. And ended up in the arms of the uniformed officer posted there.

Todd Benton's last stop that night was a jail cell.

✗

Laird Long: "Big guy, sense of humor; pounds out fiction in all genres. Has appeared in many anthologies and mystery magazines and resides in Winnipeg, Canada.

DEAD MAN'S HAND

by Steve Liskow

Andrew Dexter saw the ambulance pull away as he parked in front of his father's mansion, subtle by Fairfield County standards but still only slightly smaller than a gothic castle. The roar of a snow-blower down the driveway told him that someone, probably Travis, was already hard at work. The police cars in that driveway told him someone else was, too.

He approached the front door, snow crunching under his feet. The door opened before he could knock, a good thing, since he couldn't find his keys and didn't have a duplicate to his father's house on his spare set.

"Mr. Andrew." Sonya Torfelt stood in her maid's uniform with no expression on her face. "I'm so sorry…"

Her voice held no more emotion than he'd heard when he grew up in this house, but she used to leave a plate of cookies out for him whenever she baked. Now that he only visited occasionally, he noticed gray overtaking the brown in her hair.

He followed her through the vestibule, his wind-burned cheeks warming up until he saw two men in cheap suits in the living room. Another man in jeans and a turtleneck wrote on a label that he affixed to a plastic bag. All three towered over his five-foot-six.

"Mr. Dexter, I'm Detective Stone and this is my partner, Detective Jordan." Stone's hand engulfed his own. "And this is Dr. Edwards, the Medical Examiner."

The room looked pretty much the way it had for twenty years, the leather sofa and two armchairs matching the green of newly-minted bills. They curved around the eight-foot marble fireplace and rested on a parquet floor with a patina seasoned over the last century. The mahogany coffee table, longer than the mantel, looked ready to pounce on its clawed feet. The barrister bookcases bulged with books, and Dexter knew that his father had read every one of them more than once before his eyesight deteriorated.

"We're sorry to call you out for such bad news," Stone said.

"What happened?" Dexter asked. "You said Pop shot himself, but I can't see him doing that. That's just not…"

"Well, the maid found him sitting on the couch this morning." Stone bobbed his head toward it. "He looked like he'd been walking outside—topcoat, gloves, and scarf over his pajamas—and she says the gun in his hand was his."

"Walking?" It was coming at Dexter faster than he could handle. He'd only had one cup of coffee before they called him an hour ago.

"It was snowing like hell last night," he remembered. "And so cold…"

He hadn't slept worth a damn last night. Jessie went home because she had to finish packing for her show.

"Yeah," Stone said. "That's why we wondered about it. He was wearing slippers, and we thought that was weird, but the maid says he always wore bedroom slippers in the house and kept a pair of loafers by the back door."

"That's right." Dexter's cheeks tingled in the warm room. "He's done that as long as I can remember."

"Does this look familiar, Mr. Dexter?" Stone held up a plastic bag containing a small revolver, and Dexter forced himself to look at it.

"Uh, it could be Pop's. He had a twenty-two, kept it in his nightstand. Mom always hated it, but he kept the drawer locked when I was little."

"Is this that gun? We found a box of ammunition in the drawer upstairs, with six cartridges missing. The gun only has the one shot fired."

Dexter shook his head and it made him feel dizzy. "If there's no gun in the drawer, I suppose that's it."

"We're just kind of intrigued about a blind man having a pistol permit."

Dexter sank into the nearer chair and watched the room level off again. "He probably still has a driver's license, too. His eyes only went a couple of years ago."

"Diabetes, I understand."

Dexter saw Sonya stride through the arch with a cup and saucer on a tray. She ignored the intruders and handed it to him like he was a little kid, shivering after sledding.

"That's right. He started learning to read Braille when the doctor told him it was getting worse. That was five or six years ago. He left the brokerage firm when it got bad enough to be a problem."

"Uh-huh." Stone held up another evidence bag. "How about this?"

The coffee scalded Dexter's throat.

"I don't know what Pop's gloves looked like."

He turned the bag over in his hand so he could read the glove's label. The same maker, but four sizes larger than his own, surprising since his father was even shorter than he was.

"Was Pop wearing the left one, too?"

"Yes." Edwards took the bag back. "He was sitting on the couch with both hands in his lap. Looks like he shot himself through the right temple and died instantly."

"When you say 'looks like,' does that mean you're not sure?"

"Well," Stone said. "We're not used to a blind man walking outside in a snow storm after midnight, then coming back inside and shooting himself with a gun that he's still licensed to carry. Makes us wonder, you know?"

Dexter turned to a familiar face. "Sonya, could I have some more coffee, please? If you've made a full pot...?"

"Of course, Mr. Andrew." She disappeared through the arch again, and two technicians appeared from the central staircase across from her. Beyond it was the conservatory, where Mom used to tend her roses, but she'd been dead for—Dexter caught himself when he realized what day it was.

"Pop used to walk everywhere," he said. "When I was little, we'd go on walks all around the neighborhood. He said it helped him think. I was only six or seven, and it felt like we walked miles. Boy, did I sleep those nights."

"Sure." Stone watched the techs pick up their coats and disappear through the vestibule. "We're trying to put everything together. It looks like he was in bed for a while; the pillow has the imprint of a head and the covers are mussed up. And we found a bayberry candle in a saucer on the dresser. Burned clear down to the wick."

Stone's eyes seemed to push Dexter back in his chair. "Would you come up and look at the room for a minute, see if you notice anything?"

"You've already looked at it." Dexter saw Sonya approaching with a fresh cup and saucer on a tray. He still loved her coffee, so strong it almost dissolved his back teeth. When he reached for it, his left hand shook and he sloshed liquid into the saucer.

"Yes, but we don't know your father. You might notice something we wouldn't."

"I've already told you about the pillow." Sonya's voice rode over the snow-blower outside the window, and Dexter saw a cloud of snow blanket the shrubbery.

"Pillow?"

"Your father always slept with two pillows, Mr. Andrew. But there's only one pillow there now."

"Maybe under the bed?"

Her look made him feel eight years old again. He knew she'd have the whole living room free of fingerprint powder by the time they came back downstairs.

He followed Stone, the carpet muffling their footfalls up the stairs and down the hall, four doors on each side. Dexter remembered playing hide and seek in the twenty-nine rooms, and the servants' rooms lay on the floor above this one. Ms. Torfelt, Travis, and he wasn't sure how many others now that he no longer lived here.

Stone opened the second door on the left, and Dexter felt the temperature drop as soon as he crossed the threshold.

"Did your father always sleep with the window open?" Stone asked. "Even in this kind of weather?"

"He liked fresh air," Dexter said. "But I don't remember about winter. I haven't lived here since I went away to college, and that was eleven years ago."

The familiar furniture showcased his mother's refined taste, which Pop always trusted. Dexter recognized the rumpled queen-sized bed near the window, a beautiful roll-top desk opposite it. How could he have forgotten that desk, Pop loved it, probably worth a fortune. Now it was smudged and he knew the cops had checked this room for fingerprints, too. Another bookcase and bureau faced the foot of the bed. A melted blob filled a saucer on that bureau.

"Mom used to love bayberry candles," he said.

"Does 'used to' mean they divorced?" Stone asked. "Or is she dead, too?"

"She died." Dexter remembered the date again. "Ten years ago last night."

A heart attack, no warning. He rushed back from Harvard for her funeral, a month into his second semester. Sonya Torfelt was the glue that held him and Pop together. Barely.

Sunlight poured through the window. Outside, Travis was trundling the snow-blower back into the four-car garage, and Dexter saw the venerable Lincoln Town Car in the bay next to the riding mower.

"Do you know what time your father usually went to bed?"

"It used to be around ten, but that was a long time ago." Dexter saw a thick off-white bundle on the nightstand. "It looks like he still liked to read in bed."

"Any idea what the book is?"

"I don't read Braille." He looked under the bed, but didn't see a second pillow.

Stone studied the blob of wax. "It looks like he was in bed, then he got up again, put on his coat, and walked outside. We found indentations from the back door out to that gazebo beyond the garage. It looks like he stood there for a while, then came back inside and shot himself."

"Are you sure the footprints are his?"

"The snow stopped just after midnight, but it was too powdery to get a good impression, and the wind didn't help. All we can see is indentations. But there are small holes near them that look like he had his cane. And there was a little puddle of water under it and his shoes on the mat by the back door."

Dexter grappled with it. "But if he just came back into the living room and didn't even take off his coat and gloves, that means he took the gun out there with him. Why didn't he shoot himself outside?"

"That's another thing that bothers me." Stone ran his fingers over the Braille book. "We wondered if he was meeting someone, but there's only the one set of prints. And the servants have Sunday night off, so he could have met them inside, anyway."

Stone put the book down again. "The maid says she prepared breakfast, then realized she didn't hear the shower and went to check. Found him in the living room. She'd come down the servants' stairs to the kitchen, so she hadn't been in that part of the house before. Nobody had."

"Sonya." Dexter felt his parents' presence so strongly that he had to get out of the room. "She has a name."

Stone led the way back downstairs. "What do you do, Mr. Dexter? The maid—Sonya—said something about art."

"I'm an art dealer. Mostly contemporary painters." He met Jessie at a show three years ago.

"How's that working for you, the recession and all?"

Dexter chose his answer carefully. "Art's a good investment. It tends to appreciate, slowly but steadily. People are a little more cautious right now, but I'm holding my own."

Stone looked at his partner below them.

"We understand that your father's still worth about eleven million dollars. That's not counting the house."

The couch loomed big as a glacier. Sonya stood over the gleaming coffee table with a cloth in her hand and she gave Stone a look that could crack glass before she left. The other detective, Jordan, was looking at the pictures on the mantel as if he really cared about them. The others were gone.

"You didn't say anything about a note," Dexter said.

"We didn't find one. The maid says he saw his doctor a few weeks ago, and the chauffeur—what's his name, Travis?—the man who was clearing the driveway?—says he took him for tests last week."

Dexter remembered talking about that with Pop on Saturday, along with other even less pleasant topics.

"We're going to check with his doctor when we leave here."

Stone's eyes pushed Dexter back again. "I understand you inherit everything."

Dexter tried to keep his voice steady. "Mom's been dead for ten years and I'm the only child. I think he left a pretty generous bequest for the servants, though, especially Sonya—Ms. Torfelt. She's been with us for as long as I can remember, probably since before I was born."

"We're checking with his attorney, too." Stone looked at his notebook. "Heslin and Mackie, isn't it?"

"That's right."

Stone nodded at his notes. "I'm a little surprised he didn't go with Stiller and Epstein. They handle a lot of the big estates around here."

Dexter felt his eyes turning away from Stone's.

"Pop didn't like Jews."

"You and your father had a fight Saturday afternoon."

"Not really a fight."

"The maid—Sonya—says it was a fight. She doesn't strike me as someone who exaggerates."

"Well, I guess we did get pretty heated." Dexter felt his knees starting to shake.

"About?"

Jordan moved away from the fireplace and Dexter sank to the nearer chair again. "I told him Jessie and I have decided to get married. He almost bit my head off."

"What's her last name?" Stone looked like he already knew the answer.

"Blum."

Dexter studied the couch where his father died. "I never brought her over here again after the first time. Pop treated her like something he'd stepped in. I told him he had to understand that I wasn't just going through a phase, like teething. That's when he removed me as his executor and named Heslin instead."

"When was that?"

"Two summers ago. We knew pretty quickly that we weren't just boyfriend and girlfriend." He looked beyond the couch toward the garage, the doors now closed. The sunlight made the snow shine like diamonds and look even colder. "I've been trying to get her to move in with me, but she likes her own space, especially with the big skylight so she can paint. I told her she could keep it for her work and still live with me."

"Any particular reason you decided to marry now?"

"She's pregnant." He could see them filling the blanks with all the wrong answers and didn't mention that he was willing to convert. That was what sent Pop over the edge.

"Were you and your girlfriend together last night?"

Dexter knew they were looking for an alibi now.

"We went back to my place after dinner, but she's got a show on the west coast. She went home to finish packing. She's flying out this afternoon."

"What time did she leave, do you remember?" Neither Stone nor Jordan took a step, but Dexter felt them getting closer.

"Tennish?" He could still see Jessie after they made love, a tangle of reddish curls, that slow smile spreading across her face. When she slid from under the covers and stood naked next to the bed, she looked ten feet tall. Well, she was half a head taller than he was, but they saw eye to eye on almost everything.

"Does she know your father was planning to disinherit you?"

"It's old news. She didn't want to get married if it was going to cut me out of the will, but I'm doing okay and her paintings are starting to sell, so we won't starve.

"Besides," he continued, "she's worth more to me than money. You can get that anywhere."

"Maybe not in this economy." Stone looked at the coffee table, shiny as the snow outside. Dexter realized that he lived a half-hour from his father's house. If Jessie left him around ten, he had plenty of time to get dressed again, drive over, and kill Pop by midnight. So much for an alibi.

"You told your father that your girlfriend was pregnant."

Dexter knew he had to talk to Jessie.

"Yes. I want the baby to be mine."

"And he said he'd cut you out of the will."

"Again." Dexter forced his fingers not to clench into fists. "He said he would call his lawyer tomorrow. That would have been yesterday. Even though it was Sunday."

Stone and Jordan looked at each other again and Dexter wondered if they bought their ties at Goodwill or the Salvation Army. They looked perfect with the suits.

"Thank you, Mr. Dexter." Stone gripped Dexter's hand again. "We'll get back to you."

"When will I be able to have Pop's body?" Dexter felt like he had a bowling ball stuck in his throat.

"Probably the day after tomorrow. We'll do an autopsy, but I doubt that'll it'll turn up anything we don't already know."

Dexter ushered them through the vestibule and out the front door, the wind making his eyes tear up. He watched them drive away and turned toward the kitchen, his feet even heavier than the rest of him.

Sonya Torfelt stood by the sink, polishing a plate so assiduously that Dexter feared she would rub off the pattern. He approached the rack with the spare keys, but her voice stopped him.

"Someone will let you in when you come back, Mr. Andrew." She put the plate in the drainer, her gaze on the garage through the window.

His hand felt heavy, too. "Sonya, were there any puddles on the couch where my father died? Like the ones by his cane and shoes?"

"No." She folded the dish towel and laid it over the drainer.

"I see." He needed to be sure. "And does anyone sleep above my father's room now?"

"No." Her voice had no inflection at all, but when she turned to face him, he saw an unfamiliar twitch around her mouth. "Do you think those policemen are smart enough to look for the pillow?"

"It's hard to believe, isn't it?"

He poured himself another cup of coffee. His hand still shook when he raised it to his lips, but the warmth grew throughout his body. Maybe if he drank enough of it, it would soothe the pain. Or maybe he'd need something stronger.

Sonya watched him drain his cup before she spoke.

"Your father's lab test last week was a biopsy. He may have had lung cancer."

"Does he have the results yet?"

"Doctor Rennie was going to call him today." Her mouth twitched slightly. "If he does, it would explain his shooting himself, wouldn't it?"

"Only to someone who didn't know him." Dexter's eyes burned like someone had poured salt into them. He started to put the cup in the sink, but the woman took it from him.

"Why didn't you tell those buffoons that you're left-handed like both your parents?"

He watched her rinse the cup almost as carefully as she had the plate with his father's uneaten breakfast before he answered.

"I guess I was hoping they'd see it for themselves."

"You love her." Sonia put the cup into the drainer so delicately that he could feel her anger. "But she stole your keys to get in. And put her gloves on your father after she shot him in bed. I suppose that was so those men would find—what do they call it, gunshot residue?—if they even bothered to check."

"We don't know that, Sonya." Jessie was right-handed.

"Of course we do." The woman's eyes glittered. "The only thing we don't know is if she was stupid enough to keep the pillow with the rest of the residue and your father's blood on it. If she threw it in a trash container on the way home…"

She shook her head and her hair didn't move. "And nobody was even above her to hear the shot."

Dexter wondered how long it took Jessie to carry Pop's body down the stairs and put the coat and slippers on him before she walked outside with his cane and shoes. She was a lot bigger than Pop and she worked out.

"What if Mr. Heslin has already changed the will?"

"They'll think they have eleven million motives for me to kill Pop then, won't they?"

"Will you tell them the truth, then?"

If he closed his eyes, he could still see Jessie's face after they'd made love last night. He would never see that face again.

"Maybe if they come for me." He felt more alone than at his mother's funeral.

Sonya Torfelt turned off the coffee maker and poured detergent into the carafe.

✗

Steve Liskow (www.steveliskow.com) is a former actor, theatrical director and English teacher whose short stories have earned an Edgar nomination and the Black Orchid Novella Award. Many of his novels take place in his home state of Connecticut and feature issues including teen trafficking and a shooting at a public school. *Blood on the Tracks* (2013) introduces Detroit PI Chris "Woody" Guthrie and draws on Steve's experience as a guitarist and DJ. The book won Honorable Mention for the Writer's Digest Self-Published Novel Awards in 2014.

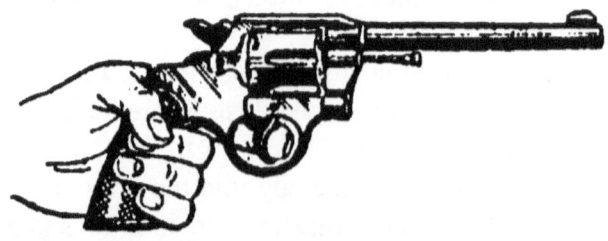

DIE, MILES CORNBLOOM

by Alex Shvartsman

The knife was stuck deep into the mesh of his screen door. It was a large kitchen knife with a serrated blade and a black plastic handle. It pinned a sheet of paper with a note written using a thick red Sharpie in large, uneven letters. The note read: "Die, Miles Cornbloom."

Up until that point, the death threats were easy to dismiss. Garbled messages on the answering machine were likely calls made to a wrong number. Vague, rambling e-mails must have been just spam. "I H8 U" spray-painted on his mailbox was surely an annoying prank by local hooligan kids. It wasn't until he found the knife and the note that Miles admitted to himself that he had a serious problem.

✗   ✗   ✗   ✗

Miles stared at the chessboard, trying to regain the advantage. Jason claimed that checkmate would come in four moves. Miles figured out how to make his friend eat those words by surviving for a whole six moves, but found no paths to victory. Jason Lam fiddled with the kitchen knife and the note, laid out on the windowsill.

"Maybe it's your job," said Jason. "You saw something in their books that they didn't want you to see, and now they're trying to scare you into staying quiet."

"You've been watching too many bad action movies. There are no dangerous secrets at my firm, and even if there were, a junior accountant like me wouldn't be privy to them." Miles reluctantly moved a rook. "The only danger I am exposed to at work is being bored to death."

"Can't argue there. Your job sure does suck." Jason advanced his knight almost immediately; it seemed that he was ready for Miles's tactic.

"So says the toll booth operator." Miles made his next play.

"At least I get to interact with people where I work," said Jason. "Mind you, that isn't always a good thing. Yesterday this guy pulls up and pays me with a totally crumpled-up ten dollar bill. Five minutes waiting in line and he couldn't find the time to straighten out his currency. Know what I did? I took his receipt and crumpled it up but good, before handing it back to the guy with his change. You should have seen the look on his face." Jason pushed a bishop. "Check."

"You do that sort of stuff, yet I'm the one getting a knife stuck into my door." Miles knocked down his king to indicate surrender. Even on a good day Jason was the better player, and today Miles's heart really wasn't in it. "No one would bother to threaten me. I'm not important enough. Look at the both of us—dead-end jobs, no families, and our Friday night is spent playing chess in my living room. This isn't exactly a recipe for getting on anyone's hit list."

"If it isn't your job, then who else could it be? Think hard, did you piss anyone off recently? Maybe cut a guy off in traffic? There are psychos out there who will stalk you for less."

"Gee, thanks Jason. You're making me feel so much better."

"I can't help it. You know I am a glass-half-empty kinda guy. So what are you going to do about it?"

"I wish I knew. I called the police and they had a couple of beat cops come by who weren't at all helpful. Told me to call them and file for a restraining order if I ever figured out who is behind this, but they wouldn't even dust the knife for fingerprints. Said it's most likely a mean prank and that they see crazy things like that all the time."

"Your tax dollars at work," said Jason. "Shameful."

✗   ✗   ✗   ✗

"**H**ey Miles, got a minute?" Laura called out as he made his way past her cubicle.

"I was just on my way out." Miles knew that tone of voice. Laura was running behind schedule again.

"It's this darn First Stanford report," she flashed him a big smile. "It needs another fifteen minutes, tops. I would totally take care of it, but I have a big date tonight and I simply must run right now if

I am to make it to the hair salon on the way home. Would you be a dear and finish it for me?"

Miles could see at a glance that there was at least an hour's worth of work still needed to complete that report. Unencumbered by family or much in a way of social obligations, he could usually be relied on to put in some late hours at the office, and his co-workers knew it. Laura was the worst offender, well aware of a small crush he had on her, and taking full advantage.

"Sorry, but I can't today. I have an appointment to keep." He left Laura pouting at her desk. In a small way, it felt good to say no. He wondered if he was becoming a terrible person.

Having managed to leave work on time, Miles went home, changed, and headed out to the self-defense class at the local gym. He signed up on a whim a week prior. He'd never been in a real fight and it'd probably be months before he learned anything that would help him in an actual altercation. Still, he found that vigorous exercise helped relieve his stress somewhat.

There was plenty of stress to cope with. Harassing phone calls, text messages, and e-mails became an unwelcome part of his life. His several visits to the precinct were a waste of time. This was New York, not some sleepy small town where nothing ever happened. Cops dealt with murder, burglary, and drugs on the daily basis and had no time for investigating vague threats; they made this abundantly clear to Miles. He had his home security upgraded. He could barely afford the payments on the new state-of-the-art alarm system, but at least it made him feel marginally better.

A loud noise intruded on Miles's troubled thoughts as he crossed the street. He turned just in time to see a beat-up white van bearing upon him at what must have been close to fifty miles per hour, running a red light. Perhaps it was the recent gym sessions that improved his reaction speed, or maybe luck was with him that evening, but Miles was able to throw himself out of the way moments before the van reached him. The van made no attempt to slow down, nor did the driver honk. It kept racing down the deserted street. Miles watched the van depart. It had no license plates.

To their credit, the cops arrived quickly. A police cruiser pulled up just as Miles finished tending to his scraped arms and legs using a bottle of water and a clean t-shirt from his gym bag. Two officers emerged from the car.

"Great," said the older cop. "It's you again."

"Let me get this straight," said the cop after listening to Miles's complaint, "you want us to find an unmarked white van with no plates, which sped down this here residential street, which has no cameras of any kind, because you imagine it was trying to run you down, to which there are no witnesses. That about right?"

Miles always had a mild fear of authority. Not the kind of well-justified anxiety a criminal might exhibit, but the sort of apprehension that comes with a suburban upbringing and lack of personal experience in dealing with law enforcement. This frame of mind allowed him to hold back the response he really wanted to give, but just barely.

"I am telling you, officer, someone out there is trying to get me," said Miles after mentally counting to ten. "I'm not crazy. I have no history of paranoid behavior. I never even dialed 911 before until these things began happening to me. I called because I didn't know what else to do, and was hoping you'd help me."

"Never met a paranoid yet who admitted to being one," muttered the older cop under his breath.

"I see now that the police aren't going to take this seriously until I am hurt, or even killed," said Miles, looking the cop straight in the eye. "And when that happens, heads are going to roll. For now, I'd like your name and badge number, which I'll record carefully so that when something does happen to me, your head will be near the top of the list."

"Look," said the younger cop, "you seem like a straight shooter. Maybe someone is after you, maybe not. Truth is, my partner is right; there isn't much we can do without more information. What you really need is a good private investigator. There is this firm I heard about that specializes in stalking cases. They're called Finn & Scheer. Look them up."

✗ ✗ ✗ ✗

"Ten thousand dollars," said Paul Finn. He was wearing an elegant suit, sitting behind a massive mahogany desk in an opulent office decorated with photos of Mr. Finn rubbing shoulders with very important people. The place was designed to make the sum he requested sound like a pittance. Except that it wasn't, not to Miles.

"I'm not sure I can afford that," he said.

"Surely, Mr. Cornbloom, your safety is worth it. In exchange for this retainer, our firm will not only identify the source of these threats but ensure that they are properly dealt with. In fact, we guarantee a successful outcome, or your money back." Mr. Finn flashed the grin of a used car salesman. "You have already made the right decision by coming to see us. All you have to do now is take the final step."

Miles decided to call Finn & Scheer when he came home from work a week after the van incident to find several of his windows broken. His pricey alarm system didn't even go off. Upon closer examination, he found that its wires were expertly cut.

"All right," said Miles. "I'll need a few days to come up with the money."

Mr. Finn's smile got even wider. He produced a stack of papers from a drawer.

"No problem. Go ahead and sign these, so we can get started."

✗ ✗ ✗ ✗

"Mr. Young will see you now," the secretary informed Miles. He spent twenty minutes in the waiting room fighting the urge to get up and leave. He kept reminding himself that he was more scared of his anonymous stalkers than of his own boss, but the internal argument was wearing thin.

"Come on in, Miles. It's good to see you," Mr. Young greeted him from behind the desk. "Sorry about the wait. I was on the phone catching up with an old golfing buddy and lost track of time. You know how it is. Anyway, what can I do for you today?"

"It's about my raise, Mr. Young," said Miles.

"A raise?" Mr. Young still had a grin of his face, but his eyes weren't smiling.

"When you hired me, you said that there would be a fifteen percent raise after a six month probation period," said Miles. "I've been here two years now, and I still get the same salary as when I started."

"Yes, well, I definitely hear you, Miles," said Mr. Young. "You are doing a bang-up job, and if anybody deserves a raise, it's you. It's just that things have been a little tough lately. You know, the economy being what it is. I'm sure that if you bring it up sometime around next summer, we should be able to do something for you."

Economy notwithstanding, Miles could think of at least two coworkers who got raises within the last year.

"I'm afraid I can't wait that long," he said, straightening up to look directly at his boss. "I accepted this job based on the expectation of that pay raise, and if I can't have it, I can't continue to work here."

Mr. Young looked flabbergasted. He clearly didn't expect such tough talk from the always amenable, mild-mannered Miles.

"You can't quit on me," pleaded Mr. Young. "This is the busiest time of the year. Besides, we wouldn't want to lose you. Surely we can come to some sort of a mutually acceptable arrangement."

"Furthermore," Miles pressed on while he had the courage, "I want that fifteen percent owed me over the last year and a half paid out as a lump sum bonus, and I want the check this week." It felt liberating to demand what he wanted instead of waiting meekly to see what might be offered. It felt good not to be afraid any more.

"If those terms are agreeable to you," Miles continued, "let's talk about my title and next year's bonus structure."

⚹　⚹　⚹　⚹

The phone call came just one day after his check was cashed. Finn & Scheer were apparently very good at what they did. Miles rushed to their office, eager to finally get some answers.

"You can relax now," said Mr. Finn. "There will be no further harassment."

"Who?" was all that Miles could manage. He could almost physically feel an immense weight being lifted off his shoulders. "Who was doing this to me?"

"This is the fun part," said Mr. Finn. "It was us. The phone calls, the knife, the white van—our firm arranged for all of it."

Miles drew breath to speak but said nothing, staring at Mr. Finn, mouth agape.

"Your shocked silence is a common reaction," observed Mr. Finn. "There are several typical responses. I much prefer this to the aggression response, where a client tries to hit me."

As far as Miles was concerned, that idea was looking pretty good. A kind of cold rage was rising within him. He had enough self-control not to lunge at Mr. Finn, but did get up from the chair, finally finding his voice.

"What kind of a low, pathetic excuse for a human being are you? You've been tormenting me, destroying my property, driving me up the wall for weeks. You've turned my entire goddamn life upside down, and for what? A lousy ten grand?"

"Please," said Mr. Finn, "your anger is justified, and to be expected. However, allow me a few moments to explain?"

Miles gritted his teeth, but listened.

"Most of us live our lives as the heroes of our own narratives. Everyone else is a supporting character. Our ambitions, our drive, are derived from the desire to achieve. Then there are an unfortunate few who seem to have lost this drive. People who aren't exactly miserable, but certainly aren't happy. People who have settled for mediocrity. People like you, Mr. Cornbloom.

"We like to think of what we do as providing a service. A jolt to your system that forces you out of the comfortable routine your life has been mired in. Forces you to act. Consider your own experiences. In just a few weeks, you've joined a gym and began leading a healthier lifestyle. You've learned to stand up to authority. You got yourself a raise at work. We did turn your life upside down, Mr. Cornbloom, and for that you should thank us."

"That is some fine rhetoric," retorted Miles. "Do any of your *clients* swallow it whole, and go on to thank you for terrorizing them? Because from where I'm standing, you are just a well-spoken thug who blackmailed me and stole my money."

"Once again, a common reaction," said Mr. Finn. "Money isn't our primary motivation. It costs a bundle to properly research the potential clients and arrange for all the... special events that nudge them out of their funk. And then there are bribes. A police officer didn't mention our firm to you by coincidence. By the time we are through, there's hardly anything left to cover the overhead."

"Cry me a river," said Miles. "I want the money paid back in full, or I'm going to the police."

Mr. Finn was unfazed. "You signed a lot of papers last time you were in this office. Some of those papers had fine print. For example, it may interest you to know that you signed a backdated document consenting to being subjected to everything you've experienced in the last month. Furthermore, all of our contractual obligations to you have been met. After all, we identified the source of your threats and made certain that all such threats have ceased. The fact that we initiated the threats in the first place is irrelevant, contractually speaking."

"I will have a lawyer go over your documents with a fine comb," promised Miles. "Even if what you say is true, I'll take this case to the media and make sure that your seedy little operation is exposed, so that you can't hurt any more people."

"There is a non-disclosure agreement you signed that would prevent you from doing that," said Mr. Finn mildly. "In any case, once you've had some time to cool down and reflect upon our conversation, I'm confident you will feel differently."

✗   ✗   ✗   ✗

Back home, Miles laid out copies of the documents he signed at Finn & Scheer, but did not begin reading them. His mind was elsewhere. He thought of the quiet, routine life he led only a few weeks back, and a different person he had become since. Could it be that his tormentors truly performed a valuable service for him? Was the newfound confidence he felt worth the pain and horror he went through? He sat there, deep in thought, as the sun set and was still there when its first few rays began to color the world outside, early next morning.

Finally, Miles got up. He collected the paperwork and put it away in his desk. He picked up a sheet of graph paper, pulled a magic marker out of a drawer and wrote: "Die, Jason Lam" across the page. Then he went into the kitchen to find his largest carving knife.

✗

Alex Shvartsman is a writer, translator and game designer from Brooklyn, NY. Over 70 of his short stories have appeared in *InterGalactic Medicine Show*, *Nature*, *Galaxy's Edge*, *Daily Science Fiction*, and many other magazines and anthologies. He won the 2014 WSFA Small Press Award for Short Fiction. He is the editor of the Unidentified Funny Objects annual anthology series of humorous SF/F. His collection, *Explaining Cthulhu to Grandma and Other Stories* released in February 2015. His website is www.alexshvartsman.com.

VOWS

by R.J. Lewis

It's a long drive from the city, especially with a stranger.

Penny for your thoughts, he said coyly.

The night that lays ahead.

Me, too! he smirked.

I'd like to wipe it off his face, but I smile and think of Vaneese. It keeps me focused.

How many men has it been? Since our wedding—

Do you Frank, take this woman, Vaneese—

On a spectacular autumn day, with golden leaves on the green grass, we were married. She was beautiful in white, with her red hair and stunning mix of French and Irish features.

In the year of our courtship, I pursued her around the world. The daughter of an aristocrat, and me with enough money to chase her, which I did until she said yes.

—to love, honor, and cherish—

A lengthy honeymoon on beautiful islands with beaches of pure white sand. We swam, ate, and made love as if it was our invention, never tiring of each other.

Until the headaches began.

The original diagnosis was in Bermuda. The local doctor insisted we fly to a hospital in South Carolina.

That's when they found the tumor.

An ugly knot of dark cells in her brain the size of a gumball. And growing.

—in sickness or in health—

We moved to New York, close to the hospital. She was a dynamo, ready to fight the annoying blob in my head, as she called it.

I was frightened. But I kept a brave face, day after day.

I would often sit up all night to watch her sleep, just to have a few more moments gazing at her.

The treatments made her hair fall out, and she became rail thin, with dark rings around her eyes, but she was still beautiful to me.

The doctors tried combinations of chemicals, radiation, and treatments more vile. Soon, they told me there was no improvement, prescribing drugs to ease the pain.

There was no more they could do.

Still, she went on, I don't know where she found the strength.

Acupuncture, nutritionists, herbalists—she went to them all. Each day her eyes grew more hollow and her hair did not return.

—for richer, for poorer—

The doctors gave her only weeks to live. Then one day, she met me at the door, and told me of someone who could cure her. The desperate look in her eyes worried me.

The woman arrived at eight. Her heavy, sexless form in a floral dress, and hair sprouting above her lip and from her ears. She was as wrinkled as an apple doll, and something about her chilled me.

She spoke with an accent from everywhere and nowhere.

There are ways, ancient ways. You will go on—but not be completely alive, she said, with the authority of an expert.

Will I look like this—Vaneese said, her hand going to her bald head.

You will be beautiful again, the old woman said. But it must be done soon. The longer you wait, the more often you will need—to feed.

Feed? I said. My question was ignored.

Then she talked money, naming an outrageous sum.

That's a lot, I said.

You must start tonight, she advised.

I put her off, telling her we would call the next day.

Once she left, I told Vaneese it was a scam, that she was one of those evil people who preyed on the unwell.

Vaneese wouldn't hear of it. It was the only argument we'd ever had. Finally, too exhausted to quarrel, we went to bed.

She died during the night.

—forsaking all others—

When I woke next to her corpse, my first call should have been to someone else—anyone. But no, I dialed the number the old woman left and begged her help, incoherent with grief.

She told me to keep the room cool until she arrived. And to get money—it was now more—a lot more, a sum that would nearly wipe me out.

I was to tell no one.

In a daze, I went to the bank and spent two hours converting stocks, bonds, and accounts into cash, which I carried out in a briefcase. Was she merely a thief? It didn't matter, without Vaneese, what use did I have of money?

As the sun sank she arrived with dirty boxes of equipment and two muscular men as ugly as herself. She went into the bedroom and began to draw pentagrams and arcane symbols on the floor.

She started a pot bubbling on a hot plate, and began to chant in a language I could not identify. I waited with the men. After several hours, as midnight approached, she ladled some of the dark mixture into a cracked porcelain mug.

Do you love your wife, Mr. Jameson? she said.

Yes, I said, my throat tight. More than life.

She nodded her wizened head. Then you will have to help her. She will need to feed often.

Feed?

She will know what to do—but first! she said with a gesture.

The two men held me with an iron grip and pulled my right hand forward.

What are you doing? I asked, as the hag pulled out a large knife.

Sh, she said, as if quieting a child. She slid the knife across my open palm, drawing blood. She led me to the bed, still in the embrace of the men. She poured the smelly brew into Vaneese's mouth, still chanting, and followed the mixture with a drop of my blood from the blade.

Eat, my dear, she cooed.

Vaneese's body twitched, as if coming awake. The woman held my hand to Vaneese's mouth, and she began to suckle the open wound. The woman chanted.

The men let me go.

I was transfixed, unable to pull away. I lay down next to her, and fell asleep as she drew blood from my hand.

How many hours we were there, I don't know. An entire day, I believe, because when we woke it was dark again. The house was cleaned of the arcane symbols, and the case with the money was gone. The cut on my hand was gone as well.

Vaneese yawned, stretched, and rose from the bed, looking the picture of health.

But she was different.

Not outwardly. She was still my dear, sweet Vaneese, but there was something behind her eyes—a fierceness.

The first change was she slept during the day and could only go out at night. I did as well, grateful just to be with her.

She also didn't eat much.

A few weeks later, she began to deteriorate, her eyes growing sunken, and her new hair turning ashen.

What can I do, I asked, more blood?

She shook her head. I know what I need. I feel it, inside, she said touching her chest. Bring me someone. It doesn't matter who.

The first one was easy. I went downtown to a known gay bar and found a man on the prowl. I told him I was just coming out and bought him drinks. Some mild cajoling, and I convinced him to come home with me.

As we arrived, I poured him a drink, and went to Vaneese hiding in the unlit bedroom.

I have him, I whispered.

She hid in a dark corner, her body different. Her eyes glowed a dark yellow, her teeth long and pointed, and her fingernails extending into claws. She wore the smell of the grave.

Yessss. Sssend him to me!

I invited the man into the bedroom.

I like it with the light on, he protested.

Vaneese leapt on top of him, he gave one yell of surprise, which became a gurgle as she ripped his throat out.

I stepped out of the room and shut the bedroom door to have a drink as Vaneese growled and ripped flesh.

As she fed.

The next morning she looked radiant as she slept. Disposing of what remained—and cleaning up—it took an effort to keep my lunch down. The blood red bones, with traces of meat fit easily into a garbage bag.

—until death do you part—

Vaneese looked sickly again today, but after tonight, she will again have weeks of good health. I was prepared, having found this young man. To be careful, I offered him a weekend at a cabin in the woods.

Another empty headed young man looking for a sugar daddy.

He rested his hand in my lap on the ride up. I haven't had to actually have sex with one of these choices, but if necessary—

Gonna be quite a night, he said rubbing me gently.

Yes, I said hoarsely, trying to behave as though overcome with lust.

Anything for Vaneese.

When we get to the cabin, it will be Vaneese he meets—and then—his maker.

I rented a car for the trip, and the young man thought nothing about the rented woodchipper I pulled in tow.

What remains of his body will not be a problem.

Not this time.

R. J. Lewis is a professional magician who performs in New York and other states. He has performed as a street performer and appeared on Broadway in *Barnum*, both onstage and in the lobby before the show (thus earning two salaries)! He also appears in NYC's longest-running magic show, "Monday Night Magic." He is just finishing a new novel and has short stories appear in anthologies edited by Marvin Kaye, including *The Ultimate Hallowe'en*. He resides with his wife in New Jersey.

SOMEWHERE BETWEEN A & B

by Steve Hagood

"I told you we shouldn't have let her go," Helen Benning shrieked. "She's only sixteen years old."

"Oh come on, Helen," her husband replied. "She was with friends. There was security."

"It's Detroit, for crying out loud!" Helen shot back.

I sighed. "Folks."

Harvey and Helen Benning sat in chairs around the table in my bar. Harvey wore round glasses and a ponytail slicked back from an expanding forehead. His wife wore too much makeup and perched on the edge of her chair. They were definitely an odd couple. He reminded me of a pothead, she Mrs. Potato Head.

Their daughter, Heather, had not returned home from a concert the night before. Helen was frantic; Harvey seemed to be in shock.

"Let's go over it again," I said.

Helen sighed and looked at me as if I were an idiot. "Heather went to a concert last night with her friends," she said in a tone that suggested that she did indeed think I was an idiot. "They went to see that one guy. What's his name, Harvey? Some kind of candy?"

"Eminem," I said.

"That's it," Helen said, snapping her attention back to me. "What kind of name is that, anyway?"

I thought about explaining, but knew she didn't care. "And she was supposed to be sleeping over at a friend's house afterwards?"

"That's right. Heather was meeting Paula Russell and Stacey Hoover at the concert and then going back to Paula's house after." Helen folded her arms across her ample chest and sat back in her chair, a scowl creasing her face. Evidently, it was now Stacey and Paula's fault that her daughter hadn't returned home. I was sure Eminem would have been relieved to learn that he had been absolved.

"What did Stacey and Paula have to say?"

"They say she never showed up," Helen said and harrumphed.

"How are you sure she did?"

"Her father dropped her off."

We both turned to Harvey. He looked stoned; maybe he was.

"Right, Harvey?" Helen said. Her tone suggested that said she had better be right.

"Well," Harvey said, stretching the word out.

"Well what?" his wife snapped. "You did take her." It wasn't a question this time.

"Sure, I drove her," Harvey said, "but she wanted to be dropped off a couple blocks away. You know how kids are; they don't want to be seen being dropped off by their old man. It isn't cool."

Helen closed her eyes and sighed. "Harvey," she moaned under her breath. Obviously, this wasn't Harvey's first screw up.

"Okay," I said before she could start in on him again. "Why come to me? Why not the police?"

I had been a detective with the Detroit Police. Following my forced retirement, I bought into the bar that we sat in.

"We went to the police," Helen said.

"And?"

"And they said they'd look into it, but they said there wasn't much they could do. One of the detectives suggested we come to you."

"And they said they couldn't do much because?"

"I don't know," Helen said, annoyed.

"Because she had run away before," I said, "and they think that's what she's done this time as well."

"How did you know that?" she asked.

The truth is that the Detroit Police Department stays pretty busy investigating shootings, robberies, rapes, and other major crimes. They don't have time for run-of-the-mill runaways, especially runaways that have run away before. Besides, I had spent ten minutes with the Bennings and I wanted to run away, but that's not what I said. Instead, I said, "I was a cop a long time. I've seen it before."

"So you won't help us, either," Helen Benning said, sitting forward and scooting to the edge of her seat.

"I didn't say that," I said, stemming the coming onslaught, "I'll see what I can find out from the friends. I'll also need a recent picture."

Helen dug in her handbag. I looked at Harvey; he was still in another world. Helen came up with a standard wallet-sized school photo and handed it to me.

I looked at it. Heather had brown hair, stylishly cut. Her makeup looked professionally applied. She could easily have passed for 21. They hadn't had girls like that when I was in high school.

I looked up from the picture to see Helen about to start in on Harvey. I had no desire to watch this woman berate her husband, so I stood and ushered them out the door.

✗ ✗ ✗ ✗

I found Stacey Hoover and Paula Russell at Paula's house in Taylor, a suburb of Detroit. They sat side by side on a sofa, across a low coffee table from where I sat in a matching armchair. Stacey was blond and her hair fell from a part above her left eye and covered the outside half of her right eye. Paula's was red and similarly styled. She sat with her hands resting on her pressed together knees. They had spent the night crammed into a relatively small room and had had noise blasted at them at a level that would probably be construed as assault, yet they still looked as fresh as the school picture of Heather Benning that I had in my pocket. What's that saying about youth being wasted on the young?

Mrs. Russell paced nervously. She had let me in because she was too polite not to, but she didn't like it.

The girls and I were embroiled in an old-fashioned pissing contest. They were good at it, and two things were becoming clear as the three of us eyed each other in silence; first, I wasn't going to get these girls to talk in front of Paula's mom, and second, Paula's mom wasn't good at the pissing contest. Her nerves were frayed and were about to supersede her manners. I was about to be back out on the street.

I cleared my throat and turned to her. "Could I trouble you for a glass of water?"

She didn't want to leave me alone with the girls, but again her manners won out.

I waited until she had left the room and then turned my attention back to the girls. "Let me see if I can guess what's going on,"

I said. "You two were supposed to cover for Heather while she hooked up with her boyfriend."

Paula's eyes widened just enough to tell me I was on the right track. I suppressed a smile. Every generation of teenagers think they've invented some great scheme for putting one over on their parents. I'm sure the reason they think that is that it works. The world is full of parents who believe their child would never lie to them. Not my child. She would never do that. Yeah right, she would never do the same thing that you did to your parents.

"I appreciate your loyalty to your friend," I continued, "but it's the oldest gag in the book. You tell your parents that you're staying at her house and she tells her parents that she's staying at your house, and then you go to an all-night party or whatever. I'm sure my parents used it when they were your age."

Paula was the weak link, her eyes drifted toward the door from which her mother would return. I didn't blame her; it would probably have been Stacey if we had been at Stacey's house.

"Where is she, Paula?"

"She's with Ryan Stevens," Paula blurted.

"Paula!" Stacey squealed.

"Shut up, Stacey," Paula said.

"Where are they, Paula?" I said before the fight could intensify.

"This motel called the Woodward Inn."

"Paula, stop," Stacey said.

"No," Paula replied. "I can't have this come back on me." She turned back to me. "Chuck, this kid at school, works there. I think his family owns it or something. He lets kids use a room if one's available—which there always is; the place is a dump."

"And this is all off the books, right? He doesn't tell his boss, just keeps the money?"

Paula gave me a look as if she couldn't believe that someone so dumb had figured out their scheme. "I don't know what he does," she said. "But if it was me, I doubt I'd tell my boss."

I smiled to indicate that I was now up to speed with their teenage shenanigans. "How'd she get there? Ryan pick her up?"

Paula shook her head. "She was supposed to meet him. She took Stacey's car."

I looked at Stacey. "Your car is missing?"

"She'll bring it back," Stacey said. There was more bluster in the statement than conviction.

"How'd you get home?" I asked.

"We called another friend to come and get us."

"You didn't call Heather?"

"We tried," Paula said. "Her cell went straight to voice mail."

"You wouldn't happen to have a picture of Ryan Stevens, would you?"

Paula rolled her eyes; I was pushing my luck. "Just in a year-book," she said.

"Can I borrow it? I'll return it when I'm done."

Paula sighed; grown-ups are such a hassle. "Will you leave if I give it to you?"

"Yes."

"Okay," she said, pushing herself up off the couch as if the weight of the world was on her shoulders.

✗　✗　✗　✗

Woodward Ave is probably the most famous street in Detroit. It hosts the annual Thanksgiving Parade and the Woodward Dream Cruise, where car buffs show off their vintage autos. Like the rest of Detroit, it has its good places and its bad places. Comerica Park, the home of the Detroit Tigers, sits on Woodward. Across the street is The Hockeytown Café, The Fox Theater, The State Theater, and the Fillmore Theater. It's one of the good places. However, the further north you travel on Woodward, the bleaker it gets. The Woodward Inn was about three miles north of The Fillmore. It wasn't Disney World, but Heather should have been able to make the ten minute drive without any problems. I did.

The motel was indeed a dump. Fifteen single-story units, desperately in need of fresh paint, sat in a squared-off U. The parking lot was empty except for three cars parked in front of the units. A weathered sign that read "Office" hung over the door in the right front corner of the U.

My tires crunched across the gravel parking lot as I pulled in and parked in front of the office. The squeak of the screen door hinges drowned out the tinkle of the bell that hung above the door.

The office was as expected. The linoleum floor had enough dirt ground into it that I might as well have been standing in the parking lot. A cigarette machine stood along one wall, next to a rack that held brochures for some of the seedier strip clubs and massage parlors in the city. A worn out couch slumped against the opposite wall inviting anyone in search of a disease to sit. Behind a sheet of bulletproof glass, ignoring me, sat a teenage boy studying one of those men's magazines that feature the latest hot celebrity in her underwear. He wore a black tee shirt that sported a hard rock band's logo and had greasy hair that covered his eyes. Little metal arrows pierced his ears. I rang the bell that sat on my side of the glass.

"Yeah, what?" he said not looking up.

"You Chuck?"

"That's right."

"I'm looking for Ryan Stevens, Chuck."

"No one here by that name," Chuck said, turning the page.

"Look at me, Chuck," I said, slamming my palm on the glass, pinning a twenty in front of his eyes.

Chuck's head jerked up. "I don't know anyone named Steven Whatever," he said. "And a twenty ain't gonna make me remember."

"I know about the scam you've got going on here," I said, "and I don't really care. However, I bet your boss and the police would. So why don't you just tell me where Ryan is, and I'll go and leave you to gawk at Paris Hilton in her underwear."

"It's not Paris Hilton," Chuck sneered.

"Whatever," I snapped, starting to tire of teenagers.

Chuck sighed. "He's over in number 12."

"Give me the key."

"Why?"

"Because you don't want to have to explain to your boss why some crazy man kicked in the door to number 12."

Chuck gave me a nasty look and reached for the key on a hook behind him. He held it up where I could see it and said, "You know, you're a real—"

"I know what I am," I said, interrupting him. "Just give me the damn key."

Number 12 occupied the far back corner. I crossed the parking lot, kicking at weeds that rose up through the gravel, hoping to find a couple of kids up to no good, but otherwise safe and sound. An SUV sat in front of the unit, but not Stacey's Ford Focus.

I knocked on the door just below the 12 that had been stenciled on sometime before I had been born. I waited a moment and then knocked again. My stomach started to twist into a knot. When still no answer came after another minute, I inserted the key, twisted the knob and pushed open the door.

The room resembled the office, dirty and worn. Threadbare carpet stretched between walls that had at one time been white, but were now a grimy gray. A pyramid of beer cans stood on the dresser in front of a mirror. A haze of beer fumes and sleep breath hung over the bed on which laid Ryan Stevens. He was a big kid, probably a football player. Maybe he threw the discus on the track team, but he was still just a kid.

He snored blissfully. A quick search of the rest of the room revealed that he was alone; Heather wasn't there. I slapped the kid's feet. "Ryan," I said, "time to get up."

The cadence of snoring didn't miss a beat. I picked up an ice bucket that sat on the dresser next to the beer can pyramid. The ice had melted. Thanking God for not having blessed me with children, I walked to the head of the bed and upended the bucket of water onto Ryan's face.

He lurched to a sitting position, spitting and sputtering. Then the 12 pack he drank the night before hit him square in the forehead. He flopped back onto the bed, holding his head and moaning.

I laughed and walked to the bathroom to retrieve a towel that matched the color of the walls. I empathized with the kid; for the first few months after my "retirement" from the police department, I woke most days feeling the same way. I dropped the towel on his head and said, "Come on, get up."

"Who are you?" he moaned from under the towel.

"My name is Chase," I said. "I'm looking for Heather Benning."

"Heather?" he said, perplexed. "She's not here."

"I can see that. Where is she?"

"I don't know. She never showed up."

"She never showed up," I echoed. "And you just left it at that?"

"No. I called her cell. Some guy answered. When I asked for Heather he laughed and said Heather was tied up and couldn't come to the phone. I called like ten times but it kept going straight to voicemail after that."

The knot in my stomach twisted a little tighter. "So you figured she stood you up for another guy and decided to drink a 12 pack by yourself."

"Yeah," Ryan moaned. "I had already paid Chuck for the room..." He paused and peeked out from under the towel. "You know about Chuck, right?"

"Yeah," I sighed. "I know about Chuck."

Ryan nodded and retreated under the towel. "Seemed like a good idea at the time."

"And now?"

The kid just moaned.

I laughed and said, "Hang in there kid." Then left him to his misery.

⚹　　⚹　　⚹　　⚹

Using my many years of experience as a detective with the Detroit Police Department, I reasoned that Heather had disappeared somewhere between point A, being The Fillmore, and point B, The Woodward Inn. So, I only had three miles and a few thousand potential witnesses to canvas.

I should have turned the investigation over to the police at that point. Something had obviously gone wrong and the police had far more resources than I did, but in just a few hours I had grown attached to the girl. I had another Heather many years before. Her name had been Cori. She, too, had gone missing and everyone, including me, had thought she'd "turn up" as well. She had turned up all right, in a shallow grave. I wasn't about to give up on Heather. One ghost was enough to live with.

I backtracked down Woodward, looking for Stacey's car. She said it was silver and had a Peace sign sticker on the bumper. I drove about a mile south, scanning the many parking lots along the way. Then I got lucky. A silver Ford Focus with a Peace sign sticker on the bumper was parked in front of a small store.

"Sure, I remember her," the old man who owned the store said, studying the picture. "Pretty little thing."

"She was here last night," I said, feeling a rush of adrenaline.

"Sure, last night." He pointed a gnarled finger. "Right over there by the uh… condoms, I guess they call 'em these days."

"What was she doing?"

"Well, she was doing what all the kids do over there: trying to get up the nerve to buy some."

"And did she?"

"No. Long about then, this young fella comes in. He walks right over and says something to her."

"What'd he say?"

"My hearing ain't quite what it used to be," the old-timer confessed. "But that girl got mad as blue blazes. She slapped him right across the face and stormed out of here."

"And the boy?"

"He followed after her. I figured it to be some sort of lovers' spat. Figured they wouldn't need the, uh… condoms."

I felt as if I'd been kicked in the stomach. If Heather and Ryan had a fight, and now he was hung over and Heather was nowhere to be found… this was not good.

"Would you remember what the boy looked like?" I asked the old man.

"I might."

I placed the yearbook I had borrowed from Paula on the counter between us and opened it. I pointed to Ryan Stevens's picture. "Is that him?"

The old man squinted at the page. "No, that ain't him. This here kid is too good lookin' to be the fella from last night."

Now what? Had Heather run into some other kid she knew and decided to take off with him and ditch Ryan? No, the old man said she had been angry when she had left. She wouldn't have left with some kid that made her angry.

"Hey!" the old man said. He was pointing at the yearbook. "This is the fella that was here last night."

I looked at the photo that appeared above the old man's thick yellow fingernail. Looking back at me was a pimply, pasty-faced kid with thick black sideburns. It looked like a mug shot.

✗   ✗   ✗   ✗

Out in the parking lot, I pulled out my cell phone and called my old partner, Ray Dryer.

"Ray," I said when he came on the phone. "I need whatever you have in the system on a kid named Kyle Richards. Looks to be about 17, attends high school in Taylor."

"Hello to you, too," Dryer said.

"Sorry, Ray," I said. "I don't have time for pleasantries."

"Okay," Ray said, picking up on my tone. "Who's Richards and what has he done?"

"Just a name that came up in a case I'm working."

"The couple that came in here this morning looking for their daughter?"

"It's just a name at this point, Ray. If he becomes more than that, you'll be the first to know."

"If he's still a juvenile, I won't have access to his file."

"I taught you how to get around that, Ray," I said. Dryer had been just a kid when he made detective and been partnered with me. I raised him as if he were my own, and taught him almost everything I knew.

"All right," he conceded, "but you'll owe me one."

"Just get it quick, Ray."

I paced in the parking lot, while waiting for Dryer to call back. There really wasn't any reason to look any further. I didn't believe she had left the car and voluntarily went with Richards. I wasn't going to find them checking out the American Art collection at the Detroit Institute of Arts, or splitting a coney platter at one of the ten or twelve Coney Island restaurants that lined Woodward.

"Kid's a punk," Dryer said when he finally called back.

"What have you got?"

"Possession and couple fights. Then he made the big time when he threatened a teacher with a knife and got expelled. Also did some time in juvie for that one."

"They do any psychological testing?"

Dryer paused, and then said, "Why?"

"Just wondering."

"What's going on, Chase?" Dryer asked.

I didn't know if I wanted to know what was going on.

✗   ✗   ✗   ✗

The house was a small, two-story bungalow, sitting on a street of similar houses built for soldiers returning home from World War II. The soldiers were all gone now, and the neighborhood had gone to seed, or maybe it was just a sign of the times.

I walked up the cracked, uneven walk to the crumbling porch. I reached over the two short steps and knocked on the screen door's wood frame. After a couple of minutes, the inside door opened.

A woman squinted out into the bright day from behind the screen. She wore a tattered bathrobe, held together at the neck with her left hand. A cigarette dangled from the corner of her mouth and she sported a serious case of bed head. It didn't take a detective of my ilk to know that she hadn't been awake long.

"Mrs. Richards?" I asked.

She scowled down at me from her perch. "If you're here about the rent—"

"I'm not here about the rent," I said. "I'm looking for Kyle."

Her scowl hardened. "How am I supposed to know where that boy is?"

"You're his mother, aren't you?"

"Who the hell are you anyway?" she spat, offended.

"My name is Chase. Your son's name came up in connection with—"

"Save your breath," Mrs. Richards said, "I've heard it all before, and I still don't know where he's at."

I dug a card out of my pocket. "If you hear from him, will you call me?"

The slamming of the door, left me standing with the card in my outstretched hand.

✗   ✗   ✗   ✗

I had no doubt that Mrs. Richards had no idea where her son was or what he was up to. However, that didn't mean that he wasn't around. I started up the car, took it once around the block, and parked several houses down from the Richards's house. I had nothing else to do, so I decided to watch the house for a while.

It wasn't too long before two boys emerged from behind the house. I figured that they had come from wherever Kyle Richards was, otherwise why would they be behind his house? I waited while they ambled down the block and turned the corner, and then I got out of the car and retraced their steps. Calf-high weeds whisked at my legs as I made my way to the back of the house.

A warped, rotting storm cellar door sat centered on the back of the house. I lifted it and peered inside. A dim light filtered up from somewhere and I heard a shuffling that could have been a rat, but I didn't think so.

I drew the nine-millimeter Beretta that I wore butt forward on my left hip and slowly descended the steps into the gloom. A single light bulb hung from the ceiling. In the weak light, huddled in the corner, was Heather Benning.

Feet flat on the floor, knees drawn up to her chest with her arms wrapped around them, she rocked and her entire body shook like a leaf. Her eyes were blackened and her face had started to swell. Tears left streaks in the dirt that had accumulated on her face.

As I neared, her eyes widened, but she wasn't looking at me; she was looking over my shoulder. I turned in time to see a glint of steel coming toward me. I had no time to move. The steel bar crashed into my right arm, just above the elbow. I flew to the left, landed on my side, and barrel-rolled away just as the bar came down again. It clanged on the cement floor, sending a spray of cement chips flying.

I bounded to my feet without knowing how. My right arm hung dead at my side, my hand empty. I had dropped the Beretta somewhere along the way.

"Who are you?" The kid from the yearbook asked, squeezing the steel bar in his grip.

"Swing first and ask questions later, huh?" I said.

The kid stalked closer, heaving another powerful swing. The steel bar whooshed past my chest, missing by inches.

"I came for the girl," I said, backing away.

"Well you're going to be disappointed then," Richards said.

"I'm pretty sure she'd like to leave now," I said, trying to figure out how to get the bar away from the kid.

"I said I'm not done with her yet. She thinks she's too good for someone like me. I'm gonna teach her different."

"I'm sure she appreciates your point of view now," I said. I bumped into something and realized that it was a steel support beam. I stayed there and let Richards stalk closer.

He let out a roar and swung. I stepped to the right, exposing the beam. The bar connected with an ear-splitting clang. The shock vibrated up the kid's arms, freezing him long enough for me to slip behind him. I took a handful of shaggy hair in my hand and used it to draw his head back, and then slam his face into the steel support beam. The bar fell from his hands, clanged onto the floor and rolled away. I swept Richards's legs out from under him; he went down in a heap. I rolled him onto his face and planted my knee in his spine.

✗　✗　✗　✗

Heather Benning healed from her injuries and seems to be fine. I guess time will tell if she's really okay.

Kyle Richards was arrested and is currently awaiting trial. He's being charged with battery and kidnapping. He's eighteen years old and facing a life sentence for the kidnapping. What a waste.

As for me, I feel good about getting one back. All too often when someone goes missing, we only find them after they're dead. Actually, I feel great. Score one for the good guys.

✗

Steve Hagood lives in Saline, Michigan with his wife Jenni. Together they have five children and a grandson. Steve's first novel *Chasing the Woodstock Baby* is available on Amazon in print and for Kindle. For more from the author check out www.stevehagood.com.

THE GREEK INTERPRETER

by Sir Arthur Conan Doyle

During my long and intimate acquaintance with Mr Sherlock Holmes I had never heard him refer to his relations, and hardly ever to his own early life. This reticence upon his part had increased the somewhat inhuman effect which he produced upon me, until sometimes I found myself regarding him as an isolated phenomenon, a brain without a heart, as deficient in human sympathy as he was preeminent in intelligence. His aversion to women and his disinclination to form new friendships were both typical of his unemotional character, but not more so than his complete suppression of every reference to his own people. I had come to believe that he was an orphan with no relatives living; but one day, to my very great surprise, he began to talk to me about his brother.

It was after tea on a summer evening, and the conversation, which had roamed in a desultory, spasmodic fashion from golf clubs to the causes of the change in the obliquity of the ecliptic, came round at last to the question of atavism and hereditary aptitudes. The point under discussion was, how far any singular gift in an individual was due to his ancestry and how far to his own early training.

"In your own case," said I, from all that you have told me, it seems obvious that your faculty of observation and your peculiar facility for deduction are due to your own systematic training."

"To some extent," he answered thoughtfully. "My ancestors were country squires, who appear to have led much the same life as is natural to their class. But, none the less, my turn that way is in my veins, and may have come with my grandmother, who was the sister of Vernet, the French artist. Art in the blood is liable to take the strangest forms."

"But how do you know that it is hereditary?"

"Because my brother Mycroft possesses it in a larger degree than I do."

This was news to me indeed. If there were another man with such singular powers in England, how was it that neither police nor public had heard of him? I put the question, with a hint that it was my companion's modesty which made him acknowledge his brother as his superior. Holmes laughed at my suggestion.

"My dear Watson," said he, "I cannot agree with those who rank modesty among the virtues. To the logician all things should be seen exactly as they are, and to underestimate one's self is as much a departure from truth as to exaggerate one's own powers. When I say, therefore, that Mycroft has better powers of observation than I, you may take it that I am speaking the exact and literal truth."

"Is he your junior?"

"Seven years my senior."

"How comes it that he is unknown?"

"Oh, he is very well known in his own circle."

"Where, then?"

"Well, in the Diogenes Club, for example."

I had never heard of the institution, and my face must have proclaimed as much, for Sherlock Homes pulled out his watch.

"The Diogenes Club is the queerest club in London, and Mycroft one of the queerest men. He's always there from quarter to five to twenty to eight. It's six now, so if you care for a stroll this beautiful evening I shall be very happy to introduce you to two curiosities."

Five minutes later we were in the street, walking towards Regent's Circus.

"You wonder," said my companion, "why it is that Mycroft does not use his powers for detective work. He is incapable of it."

"But I thought you said—"

"I said that he was my superior in observation and deduction. If the art of the detective began and ended in reasoning from an armchair, my brother would be the greatest criminal agent that ever lived. But he has no ambition and no energy. He will not even go out of his way to verify his own solutions, and would rather be considered wrong than take the trouble to prove himself right. Again and again I have taken a problem to him, and have received an explanation which has afterwards proved to be the correct one. And yet he was absolutely incapable of working out the practical points which must be gone into before a case could be laid before a judge or jury."

"It is not his profession, then?"

"By no means. What is to me a means of livelihood is to him the merest hobby of a dilettante. He has an extraordinary faculty for figures, and audits the books in some of the government departments. Mycroft lodges in Pall Mall, and he walks round the corner into Whitehall every morning and back every evening. From year's end to year's end he takes no other exercise, and is seen nowhere else, except only in the Diogenes Club, which is just opposite his rooms."

"I cannot recall the name."

"Very likely not. There are many men in London, you know, who, some from shyness, some from misanthropy, have no wish for the company of their fellows. Yet they are not averse to comfortable chairs and the latest periodicals. It is for the convenience of these that the Diogenes Club was started, and it now contains the most unsociable and unclubable men in town. No member is permitted to take the least notice of any other one. Save in the Stranger's Room, no talking is, under any circumstances, allowed, and three offences, if brought to the notice of the committee, render the talker liable to expulsion. My brother was one of the founders, and I have myself found it a very soothing atmosphere."

We had reached Pall Mall as we talked, and were walking down it from the St. James's end. Sherlock Holmes stopped at a door some little distance from the Carlton, and, cautioning me not to speak, he led the way into the hall. Through the glass panelling I caught a glimpse of a large and luxurious room, in which a considerable number of men were sitting about and reading papers, each in his own little nook. Holmes showed me into a small chamber which looked out into Pall Mall, and then, leaving me for a minute, he came back with a companion whom I knew could only be his brother.

Mycroft Holmes was a much larger and stouter man than Sherlock. His body was absolutely corpulent, but his face, though massive, had preserved something of the sharpness of expression which was so remarkable in that of his brother. His eyes, which were of a peculiarly light, watery grey, seemed to always retain that far-away, introspective look which I had only observed in Sherlock's when he was exerting his full powers.

"I am glad to meet you, sir," said he, putting out a broad, fat hand like the flipper of a seal. "I hear of Sherlock everywhere since you became his chronicler. By the way, Sherlock, I expected to see you round last week to consult me over that Manor House case. I thought you might be a little out of your depth."

"No, I solved it," said my friend, smiling.

"It was Adams, of course."

"Yes, it was Adams."

"I was sure of it from the first." The two sat down together in the bow-window of the club. "To anyone who wishes to study mankind this is the spot," said Mycroft. "Look at the magnificent types! Look at these two men who are coming towards us, for example."

"The billiard-marker and the other?"

"Precisely. What do you make of the other?"

The two men had stopped opposite the window. Some chalk marks over the waistcoat pocket were the only signs of billiards which I could see in one of them. The other was a very small, dark fellow, with his hat pushed back and several packages under his arm.

"An old soldier, I perceive," said Sherlock.

"And very recently discharged," remarked the brother.

"Served in India, I see."

"And a non-commissioned officer."

"Royal Artillery, I fancy," said Sherlock.

"And a widower."

"But with a child."

"Children, my dear boy, children."

"Come," said I, laughing, this is a little too much."

"Surely," answered Holmes, "it is not hard to say that a man with that bearing, expression of authority, and sun-baked skin, is a soldier, is more than a private, and is not long from India."

"That he has not left the service long is shown by his still wearing his ammunition boots, as they are called," observed Mycroft.

"He had not the cavalry stride, yet he wore his hat on one side, as is shown by the lighter skin on that side of his brow. His weight is against his being a sapper. He is in the artillery."

"Then, of course, his complete mourning shows that he has lost someone very dear. The fact that he is doing his own shopping looks as though it were his wife. He has been buying things for children, you perceive. There is a rattle, which shows that one of them is very young. The wife probably died in childbed. The fact that he has a picture-book under his arm shows that there is another child to be thought of."

I began to understand what my friend meant when he said that his brother possessed even keener faculties than he did himself. He glanced across at me and smiled. Mycroft took snuff from a tortoise-shell box and brushed away the wandering grains from his coat front with a large, red silk handkerchief.

"By the way, Sherlock," said he, I have had something quite after your own heart—a most singular problem—submitted to my judgment. I really had not the energy to follow it up save in a very incomplete fashion, but it gave me a basis for some pleasing speculations. If you would care to hear the facts—"

"My dear Mycroft, I should be delighted."

The brother scribbled a note upon a leaf of his pocket-book, and, ringing the bell, he handed it to the waiter.

"I have asked Mr Melas to step across," said he. "He lodges on the floor above me, and I have some slight acquaintance with him, which led him to come to me in his perplexity. Mr Melas is a Greek by extraction, as I understand, and he is a remarkable linguist. He earns his living partly as interpreter in the law courts and partly by acting as guide to any wealthy Orientals who may visit the Northumberland Avenue hotels. I think I will leave him to tell his very remarkable experience in his own fashion."

A few minutes later we were joined by a short, stout man whose olive face and coal black hair proclaimed his Southern origin, though his speech was that of an educated Englishman. He shook hands eagerly with Sherlock Holmes, and his dark eyes sparkled with pleasure when he understood that the specialist was anxious to hear his story.

"I do not believe that the police credit me—on my word, I do not," said he in a wailing voice. "Just because they have never heard of it before, they think that such a thing cannot be. But I know that I shall never be easy in my mind until I know what has become of my poor man with the sticking-plaster upon his face."

"I am all attention," said Sherlock Holmes.

"This is Wednesday evening," said Mr Melas. "Well, then, it was Monday night—only two days ago, you understand—that all this happened. I am an interpreter, as perhaps my neighbour there has told you. I interpret all languages—or nearly all—but as I am a Greek by birth and with a Grecian name, it is with that particular tongue that I am principally associated. For many years I have been the chief Greek interpreter in London, and my name is very well known in the hotels.

"It happens not unfrequently that I am sent for at strange hours by foreigners who get into difficulties, or by travellers who arrive late and wish my services. I was not surprised, therefore, on Monday night when a Mr Latimer, a very fashionably dressed young man, came up to my rooms and asked me to accompany him in a cab which was waiting at the door. A Greek friend had come to see him upon business, he said, and as he could speak nothing but his own tongue, the services of an interpreter were indispensable. He gave me to understand that his house was some little distance off, in Kensington, and he seemed to be in a great hurry, bustling me rapidly into the cab when we had descended to the street.

"I say into the cab, but I soon became doubtful as to whether it was not a carriage in which I found myself. It was certainly more roomy than the ordinary four-wheeled disgrace to London, and the fittings, though frayed, were of rich quality. Mr Latimer seated himself opposite to me and we started off through Charing Cross and up the Shaftesbury Avenue. We had come out upon Oxford Street and I had ventured some remark as to this being a round-about way to Kensington, when my words were arrested by the extraordinary conduct of my companion.

"He began by drawing a most formidable-looking bludgeon loaded with lead from his pocket, and switching it backward and forward several times, as if to test its weight and strength. Then he placed it without a word upon the seat beside him. Having done this, he drew up the windows on each side, and I found to my astonishment that they were covered with paper so as to prevent my seeing through them.

"'I am sorry to cut off your view, Mr Melas,' said he. 'The fact is that I have no intention that you should see what the place is to which we are driving. It might possibly be inconvenient to me if you could find your way there again.'

"As you can imagine, I was utterly taken aback by such an address. My companion was a powerful, broad-shouldered young fellow, and, apart from the weapon, I should not have had the slightest chance in a struggle with him.

"'This is very extraordinary conduct, Mr Latimer,' I stammered. 'You must be aware that what you are doing is quite illegal.'"

"'It is somewhat of a liberty, no doubt,' said he, 'but we'll make it up to you. I must warn you, however, Mr Melas, that if at any time to-night you attempt to raise an alarm or do anything which is against my interest, you will find it a very serious thing. I beg you to remember that no one knows where you are, and that, whether you are in this carriage or in my house, you are equally in my power.'

"His words were quiet, but he had a rasping way of saying them, which was very menacing. I sat in silence wondering what on earth could be his reason for kidnapping me in this extraordinary fashion. Whatever it might be, it was perfectly clear that there was no possible use in my resisting, and that I could only wait to see what might befall.

"For nearly two hours we drove without my having the least clue as to where we were going. Sometimes the rattle of the stones told of a paved causeway, and at others our smooth, silent course suggested asphalt; but, save by this variation in sound, there was nothing at all which could in the remotest way help me to form a guess as to where we were. The paper over each window was impenetrable to light, and a blue curtain was drawn across the glass-work in front. It was a quarter-past seven when we left Pall Mall, and my watch showed me that it was ten minutes to nine when we at last came to a standstill. My companion let down the window, and I caught a glimpse of a low, arched doorway with a lamp burning above it. As I was hurried from the carriage it swung open, and I found myself inside the house, with a vague impression of a lawn and trees on each side of me as I entered. Whether these were private grounds, however, or bona-fide country was more than I could possibly venture to say.

"There was a coloured gas-lamp inside which was turned so low that I could see little save that the hall was of some size and hung with pictures. In the dim light I could make out that the person who had opened the door was a small, mean-looking, middle-aged man with rounded shoulders. As he turned towards us the glint of the light showed me that he was wearing glasses.

"'Is this Mr Melas, Harold?' said he.

"'Yes.'

"'Well done, well done! No ill-will, Mr Melas, I hope, but we could not get on without you. If you deal fair with us you'll not regret it, but if you try any tricks, God help you!' He spoke in a nervous, jerky fashion, and with little giggling laughs in between, but somehow he impressed me with fear more than the other.

"'What do you want with me?' I asked.

"'Only to ask a few questions of a Greek gentleman who is visiting us, and to let us have the answers. But say no more than you are told to say, or'—here came the nervous giggle again—'you had better never have been born.'

"As he spoke he opened a door and showed the way into a room which appeared to be very richly furnished, but again the only light was afforded by a single lamp half-turned down. The chamber was certainly large, and the way in which my feet sank into the carpet as I stepped across it told me of its richness. I caught glimpses of velvet chairs, a high white marble mantelpiece, and what seemed to be a suit of Japanese armour at one side of it. There was a chair just under the lamp, and the elderly man motioned that I should sit in it. The younger had left us, but he suddenly returned through another door, leading with him a gentleman clad in some sort of loose dressing-gown who moved slowly towards us. As he came into the circle of dim light which enabled me to see him more clearly I was thrilled with horror at his appearance. He was deadly pale and terribly emaciated, with the protruding, brilliant eyes of a man whose spirit was greater than his strength. But what shocked me more than any signs of physical weakness was that his face was grotesquely criss-crossed with sticking-plaster, and that one large pad of it was fastened over his mouth.

"'Have you the slate, Harold?' cried the older man, as this strange being fell rather than sat down into a chair. 'Are his hands loose? Now, then, give him the pencil. You are to ask the questions, Mr Melas, and he will write the answers. Ask him first of all whether he is prepared to sign the papers?'

"The man's eyes flashed fire.

"'Never!' he wrote in Greek upon the slate.

"'On no conditions?' I asked at the bidding of our tyrant.

"'Only if I see her married in my presence by a Greek priest whom I know.'

"The man giggled in his venomous way.

"'You know what awaits you, then?'

"'I care nothing for myself.'

"These are samples of the questions and answers which made up our strange half-spoken, half-written conversation. Again and again I had to ask him whether he would give in and sign the documents. Again and again I had the same indignant reply. But soon a happy thought came to me. I took to adding on little sentences of my own to each question, innocent ones at first, to test whether either of our companions knew anything of the matter, and then, as I found that they showed no sign I played a more dangerous game. Our conversation ran something like this:

"'You can do no good by this obstinacy. Who are you?'

"'I care not. I am a stranger in London.'

"'Your fate will be on your own head. How long have you been here?'

"'Let it be so. Three weeks.'

"'The property can never be yours. What ails you?'

"'It shall not go to villains. They are starving me.'

"'You shall go free if you sign. What house is this?'

"'I will never sign. I do not know.'

"'You are not doing her any service. What is your name?'

"'Let me hear her say so. Kratides.'

"'You shall see her if you sign. Where are you from?'

"'Then I shall never see her. Athens.'

"Another five minutes, Mr Holmes, and I should have wormed out the whole story under their very noses. My very next question might have cleared the matter up, but at that instant the door opened and a woman stepped into the room. I could not see her clearly enough to know more than that she was tall and graceful, with black hair, and clad in some sort of loose white gown.

"'Harold,' said she, speaking English with a broken accent. 'I could not stay away longer. It is so lonely up there with only—Oh, my God, it is Paul!'

"These last words were in Greek, and at the same instant the man with a convulsive effort tore the plaster from his lips, and screaming out 'Sophy! Sophy!' rushed into the woman's arms. Their embrace was but for an instant, however, for the younger man seized the woman and pushed her out of the room, while the elder easily overpowered his emaciated victim and dragged him away through the other door. For a moment I was left alone in the room, and I sprang to my feet with some vague idea that I might in some way get a clue to what this house was in which I found myself. Fortunately, however, I took no steps, for looking up I saw that the older man was standing in the doorway, with his eyes fixed upon me.

"'That will do, Mr Melas,' said he. 'You perceive that we have taken you into our confidence over some very private business. We should not have troubled you, only that our friend who speaks Greek and who began these negotiations has been forced to return to the East. It was quite necessary for us to find someone to take his place, and we were fortunate in hearing of your powers.'

"I bowed.

"'There are five sovereigns here,' said he, walking up to me, 'which will, I hope, be a sufficient fee. But remember,' he added, tapping me lightly on the chest and giggling, 'if you speak to a human soul about this—one human soul, mind—well, may God have mercy upon your soul!'

"I cannot tell you the loathing and horror with which this insignificant-looking man inspired me. I could see him better now as the lamp-light shone upon him. His features were peaky and sallow, and his little pointed beard was thready and ill-nourished. He pushed his face forward as he spoke and his lips and eyelids were continually twitching like a man with St. Vitus's dance. I could not help thinking that his strange, catchy little laugh was also a symptom of some nervous malady. The terror of his face lay in his eyes, however, steel grey, and glistening coldly with a malignant, inexorable cruelty in their depths.

"'We shall know if you speak of this,' said he. 'We have our own means of information. Now you will find the carriage waiting, and my friend will see you on your way.'

"I was hurried through the hall and into the vehicle, again obtaining that momentary glimpse of trees and a garden. Mr Latimer followed closely at my heels and took his place opposite to me without a word. In silence we again drove for an interminable distance with the windows raised, until at last, just after midnight, the carriage pulled up.

"'You will get down here, Mr Melas,' said my companion. 'I am sorry to leave you so far from your house, but there is no alternative. Any attempt upon your part to follow the carriage can only end in injury to yourself.'

"He opened the door as he spoke, and I had hardly time to spring out when the coachman lashed the horse and the carriage rattled away. I looked around me in astonishment. I was on some sort of a heathy common mottled over with dark clumps of furze-bushes. Far away stretched a line of houses, with a light here and there in the upper windows. On the other side I saw the red signal-lamps of a railway.

"The carriage which had brought me was already out of sight. I stood gazing round and wondering where on earth I might be, when I saw someone coming towards me in the darkness. As he came up to me I made out that he was a railway porter.

"'Can you tell me what place this is?' I asked.

"'Wandsworth Common,' said he.

"'Can I get a train into town?'

"'If you walk on a mile or so to Clapham Junction,' said he, 'you'll just be in time for the last to Victoria.'

"So that was the end of my adventure, Mr Holmes. I do not know where I was, nor whom I spoke with, nor anything save what I have told you. But I know that there is foul play going on, and I want to help that unhappy man if I can. I told the whole story to Mr Mycroft Holmes next morning, and subsequently to the police."

We all sat in silence for some little time after listening to this extraordinary narrative. Then Sherlock looked across at his brother.

"Any steps?" he asked.

Mycroft picked up the *Daily News*, which was lying on the side-table.

"Anybody supplying any information as to the whereabouts of a Greek gentleman named Paul Kratides, from Athens, who is unable to speak English, will be rewarded. A similar reward paid to anyone giving information about a Greek lady whose first name is Sophy. X 2473.

"That was in all the dailies. No answer."

"How about the Greek legation?"

"I have inquired. They know nothing."

"A wire to the head of the Athens police, then?"

"Sherlock has all the energy of the family," said Mycroft, turning to me. "Well, you take the case up by all means and let me know if you do any good."

"Certainly," answered my friend, rising from his chair. "I'll let you know, and Mr Melas also. In the meantime, Mr Melas, I should certainly be on my guard if I were you, for of course they must know through these advertisements that you have betrayed them."

As we walked home together, Holmes stopped at a telegraph office and sent off several wires.

"You see, Watson," he remarked, "our evening has been by no means wasted. Some of my most interesting cases have come to me in this way through Mycroft. The problem which we have just listened to, although it can admit of but one explanation, has still some distinguishing features."

"You have hopes of solving it?"

"Well, knowing as much as we do, it will be singular indeed if we fail to discover the rest. You must yourself have formed some theory which will explain the facts to which we have listened."

"In a vague way, yes."

"What was your idea, then?"

"It seemed to me to be obvious that this Greek girl had been carried off by the young Englishman named Harold Latimer."

"Carried off from where?"

"Athens, perhaps."

Sherlock Holmes shook his head. "This young man could not talk a word of Greek. The lady could talk English fairly well. Inference—that she had been in England some little time, but he had not been in Greece."

"Well, then, we will presume that she had once come on a visit to England, and that this Harold had persuaded her to fly with him."

"That is more probable."

"Then the brother—for that, I fancy, must be the relationship—comes over from Greece to interfere. He imprudently puts himself into the power of the young man and his older associate. They seize him and use violence towards him in order to make him sign some papers to make over the girl's fortune of which he may be trustee—to them. This he refuses to do. In order to negotiate with him they have to get an interpreter, and they pitch upon this Mr Melas, having used some other one before. The girl is not told of the arrival of her brother and finds it out by the merest accident."

"Excellent, Watson!" cried Holmes. "I really fancy that you are not far from the truth. You see that we hold all the cards, and we have only to fear some sudden act of violence on their part. If they give us time we must have them."

"But how can we find where this house lies?"

"Well, if our conjecture is correct and the girl's name is or was Sophy Kratides, we should have no difficulty in tracing her. That must be our main hope, for the brother is, of course, a complete stranger. It is clear that some time has elapsed since this Harold established these relations with the girl—some weeks at any rate—since the brother in Greece has had time to hear of it and come across. If they have been living in the same place during this time, it is probable that we shall have some answer to Mycroft's advertisement."

We had reached our house in Baker Street while we had been talking. Holmes ascended the stair first, and as he opened the door of our room he gave a start of surprise. Looking over his shoulder, I was equally astonished. His brother Mycroft was sitting smoking in the armchair.

"Come in, Sherlock! Come in, sir," said he blandly, smiling at our surprised faces. "You don't expect such energy from me do you, Sherlock? But somehow this case attracts me."

"How did you get here?"

"I passed you in a hansom."

"There has been some new development?"

"I had an answer to my advertisement."

"Ah!"

"Yes, it came within a few minutes of your leaving."

"And to what effect?"

Mycroft Holmes took out a sheet of paper.

"Here it is," said he, "written with a J pen on royal cream paper by a middle-aged man with a weak constitution.

"Sir [he says]: In answer to your advertisement of to-day's date, I beg to inform you that I know the young lady in question very well. If you should care to call upon me I could give you some particulars as to her painful history. She is living at present at The Myrtles, Beckenham.

"Yours faithfully, J. DAVENPORT.

"He writes from Lower Brixton," said Mycroft Holmes. "Do you not think that we might drive to him now, Sherlock, and learn these particulars?"

"My dear Mycroft, the brother's life is more valuable than the sister's story. I think we should call at Scotland Yard for Inspector Gregson and go straight out to Beckenham. We know that a man is being done to death, and every hour may be vital."

"Better pick up Mr Melas on our way," I suggested. "We may need an interpreter."

"Excellent," said Sherlock Holmes. "Send the boy for a four-wheeler, and we shall be off at once." He opened the table-drawer as he spoke, and I noticed that he slipped his revolver into his pocket. "Yes," said he in answer to my glance, "I should say, from what we have heard, that we are dealing with a particularly danger-ous gang."

It was almost dark before we found ourselves in Pall Mall, at the rooms of Mr Melas. A gentleman had just called for him, and he was gone.

"Can you tell me where?" asked Mycroft Holmes.

"I don't know, sir," answered the woman who had opened the door; "I only know that he drove away with the gentleman in a carriage."

"Did the gentleman give a name?"

"No, sir."

"He wasn't a tall, handsome, dark young man?"

"Oh, no, sir. He was a little gentleman, with glasses, thin in the face, but very pleasant in his ways, for he was laughing all the time that he was talking."

"Come along!" cried Sherlock Holmes abruptly. "This grows serious," he observed as we drove to Scotland Yard. "These men have got hold of Melas again. He is a man of no physical courage, as they are well aware from their experience the other night. This villain was able to terrorize him the instant that he got into his presence. No doubt they want his professional services, but, having used him, they may be inclined to punish him for what they will regard as his treachery."

Our hope was that, by taking train, we might get to Beckenham as soon as or sooner than the carriage. On reaching Scotland Yard, however, it was more than an hour before we could get Inspector Gregson and comply with the legal formalities which would enable us to enter the house. It was a quarter to ten before we reached London Bridge, and half past before the four of us alighted on the Beckenham platform. A drive of half a mile brought us to The Myrtles—a large, dark house standing back from the road in its own grounds. Here we dismissed our cab and made our way up the drive together.

"The windows are all dark," remarked the inspector. "The house seems deserted."

"Our birds are flown and the nest empty," said Holmes.

"Why do you say so?"

"A carriage heavily loaded with luggage has passed out during the last hour."

The inspector laughed. "I saw the wheel-tracks in the light of the gate-lamp, but where does the luggage come in?"

"You may have observed the same wheel-tracks going the other way. But the outward-bound ones were very much deeper—so much so that we can say for a certainty that there was a very considerable weight on the carriage."

"You get a trifle beyond me there," said the inspector, shrugging his shoulders. "It will not be an easy door to force, but we will try if we cannot make someone hear us."

He hammered loudly at the knocker and pulled at the bell, but without any success. Holmes had slipped away, but he came back in a few minutes. "I have a window open," said he.

"It is a mercy that you are on the side of the force, and not against it, Mr Holmes," remarked the inspector as he noted the clever way in which my friend had forced back the catch. "Well, I think that under the circumstances we may enter without an invitation."

One after the other we made our way into a large apartment, which was evidently that in which Mr Melas had found himself. The inspector had lit his lantern, and by its light we could see the two doors, the curtain, the lamp, and the suit of Japanese mail as he had described them. On the table lay two glasses, an empty brandy-bottle, and the remains of a meal.

"What is that?" asked Holmes suddenly.

We all stood still and listened. A low moaning sound was coming from somewhere over our heads. Holmes rushed to the door and out into the hall. The dismal noise came from upstairs. He dashed up, the inspector and I at his heels, while his brother Mycroft followed as quickly as his great bulk would permit.

Three doors faced us upon the second floor, and it was from the central of these that the sinister sounds were issuing, sinking sometimes into a dull mumble and rising again into a shrill whine. It was locked, but the key had been left on the outside. Holmes flung open the door and rushed in, but he was out again in an instant, with his hand to his throat.

"It's charcoal," he cried. "Give it time. It will clear."

Peering in, we could see that the only light in the room came from a dull blue flame which flickered from a small brass tripod in the centre. It threw a livid unnatural circle upon the floor, while in the shadows beyond we saw the vague loom of two figures which crouched against the wall. From the open door there reeked a horrible poisonous exhalation which set us gasping and coughing. Holmes rushed to the top of the stairs to draw in the fresh air, and then, dashing into the room, he threw up the window and hurled the brazen tripod out into the garden.

"We can enter in a minute," he gasped, darting out again. "Where is a candle? I doubt if we could strike a match in that atmosphere. Hold the light at the door and we shall get them out, Mycroft, now!"

With a rush we got to the poisoned men and dragged them out into the well-lit hall. Both of them were blue-lipped and insensible, with swollen, congested faces and protruding eyes. Indeed, so distorted were their features that, save for his black beard and stout figure, we might have failed to recognize in one of them the Greek interpreter who had parted from us only a few hours before at the Diogenes Club. His hands and feet were securely strapped together, and he bore over one eye the marks of a violent blow. The other, who was secured in a similar fashion was a tall man in the last stage of emaciation, with several strips of sticking-plaster arranged in a grotesque pattern over his face. He had ceased to moan as we laid him down, and a glance showed me that for him at least our aid had come too late. Mr Melas, however, still lived, and in less than an hour, with the aid of ammonia and brandy, I had the satisfaction of seeing him open his eyes, and of knowing that my hand had drawn him back from that dark valley in which all paths meet.

It was a simple story which he had to tell, and one which did but confirm our own deductions. His visitor, on entering his rooms, had drawn a life-preserver from his sleeve, and had so impressed him with the fear of instant and inevitable death that he had kidnapped him for the second time. Indeed, it was almost mesmeric, the effect which this giggling ruffian had produced upon the unfortunate linguist, for he could not speak of him save with trembling hands and a blanched cheek. He had been taken swiftly to Beckenham, and had acted as interpreter in a second interview, even more dramatic than the first, in which the two Englishmen had menaced their prisoner with instant death if he did not comply with their demands. Finally, finding him proof against every threat, they had hurled him back into his prison and after reproaching Melas with his treachery, which appeared from the newspaper advertisement, they had stunned him with a blow from a stick, and he remembered nothing more until he found us bending over him.

And this was the singular case of the Grecian Interpreter, the explanation of which is still involved in some mystery. We were able to find out, by communicating with the gentleman who had answered the advertisement, that the unfortunate young lady came of a wealthy Grecian family, and that she had been on a visit to some friends in England. While there she had met a young man named Harold Latimer, who had acquired an ascendency over her and had eventually persuaded her to fly with him. Her friends, shocked at the event, had contented themselves with informing her brother at Athens, and had then washed their hands of the matter. The brother, on his arrival in England, had imprudently placed himself in the power of Latimer and of his associate, whose name was Wilson Kemp—a man of the foulest antecedents. These two, finding that through his ignorance of the language he was helpless in their hands, had kept him a prisoner, and had endeavoured by cruelty and starvation to make him sign away his own and his sister's property. They had kept him in the house without the girl's knowledge, and the plaster over the face had been for the purpose of making recognition difficult in case she should ever catch a glimpse of him. Her feminine perceptions, however, had instantly seen through the disguise when, on the occasion of the interpreter's visit, she had seen him for the first time. The poor girl, however, was herself a prisoner, for there was no one about the house except the man who acted as coachman, and his wife, both of whom were tools of the conspirators. Finding that their secret was out, and that their prisoner was not to be coerced, the two villains with the girl had fled away at a few hours' notice from the furnished house which they had hired, having first, as they thought, taken vengeance both upon the man who had defied and the one who had betrayed them.

Months afterwards, a curious newspaper cutting reached us from Buda-Pesth. It told how two Englishmen who had been travelling with a woman had met with a tragic end. They had each been stabbed, it seems, and the Hungarian police were of opinion that they had quarrelled and had inflicted mortal injuries upon each other. Holmes, however, is, I fancy, of a different way of thinking, and he holds to this day that, if one could find the Grecian girl, one might learn how the wrongs of herself and her brother came to be avenged.